PENGUIN B

FATHER DA

Nick Papandreou was born in 1956 in Berkeley, California. He received a BA and a Ph.D. in economics from Yale and Princeton respectively, and subsequently he studied literature at Vermont College and Norwich University. Between 1989 and 1991 he worked as an economist at the World Bank. His fiction has appeared in *Harvard Review*, *Quarry Magazine* and *Quarterly West*, and he is also the author of a play. He now lives in Athens and writes full-time. *Father Dancing* is his first book.

Father Dancing

NICK PAPANDREOU

PENGUIN BOOKS

PENGUIN BOOKS

Published by the Penguin Group
Penguin Books Ltd, 27 Wrights Lane, London W8 5TZ, England
Penguin Books USA Inc., 375 Hudson Street, New York, New York 10014, USA
Penguin Books Australia Ltd, Ringwood, Victoria, Australia
Penguin Books Canada Ltd, 10 Alcorn Avenue, Toronto, Ontario, Canada M4V 3B2
Penguin Books (NZ) Ltd, 182–190 Wairau Road, Auckland 10, New Zealand

Penguin Books Ltd, Registered Offices: Harmondsworth, Middlesex, England

First published by Viking 1996
Published in Penguin Books 1997
1 3 5 7 9 10 8 6 4 2

Printed in England by Clays Ltd, St Ives plc

To my sister Sophia
and to our grandmother

I would like to thank my friend George Levounis for his sharp comments and intelligent suggestions, Thanasis Niarchos and Christophoros Liontakis for their attention to language, Vassilis Vassilikos for his continual encouragement, Thanasis Kastaniotis, my Greek publisher, for his support, and Hugh Barnes of Penguin for his patience and faith.

Certain members of my family thought that this book was about them, but when they read it, barely recalled a thing. Perhaps it's because creative memories have their own stories to tell.

Contents

1 *A Crowded Heart*

To describe Greece I would share with you a tomato on the sandy beaches of Skopellos, open a sea-urchin with my penknife and serve you the scarlet eggs inside while the salt stretches the skin on our backs. We would bodysurf on white waves in the day and soak up the moonlight at night. I would dry you a starfish and hang it on your wall so you could smell the salty Aegean in your room, and ask you to breathe in the aroma of osier, broom and ginger root. I would teach you the games of *mountzouri* and *gourouna* and how to sit in the lap of a cactus without getting any needles under your skin; we would listen to Byzantine hymns from the church of Saint Christopher, inhale frankincense, kiss the hand of an old priest, and suck honey from wax.

To know my Greece I would take you to my grandfather's village in the Erymanthean Mountains, where Hercules caught the wild boar, and translate while an eighty-year-old woman in black tells you how my grandfather came into this world after a difficult birth, nearly strangled by his own umbilical cord, and how he emerged victorious carrying a rose in his hand and the midwife laid a fig between his legs to

I

make him smell sweet and attract the women when he grew older.

I would take you to the island of Chios across from Turkey, where my father was born, and show you walls pocked by Turkish guns. My childhood memories of my father are of a man at a distance. I don't recall the smell of his shaving lotion, the shape of his hands, or the way he wore his hat. Instead I see him being carried on the shoulders of Greek villagers, I see his solitary form on a balcony, I see him surrounded by crowds, lost in their embrace.

I would tell you about the way he seemed to know what the crowd was thinking and about his ability to push these thoughts one step further. I'd show you the spacious halls of Maximou – the offices of the Greek prime minister – where he resided in the 1980s and the 1990s and then let you pick someone at random from the streets of Athens to tell you why he or she hates him or loves him.

Once, when my father was very sick, a man with a picture of my father taped to his chest found me in the kitchen of our home and handed me what looked like a butcher's shopping list. In fact, it was sort of a legal document:

I, the undersigned, promise to provide the chief with the following:

> 1 liver
> 1 heart
> 1 lung
> 1 kidney
> 1 small or 1 large intestine

1 leg (not the right one which has two scars)

and to cooperate with the doctors chosen to act upon my body.

I would teach you how to recognize a special breed of person, the fanatic, to pick him out in a crowd by his unswerving gaze, the way he walks in a silent zone of empty space. I can sniff his sweaty anxiety from a distance. The fanatic is the one who suffocates you in his embrace and grabs your crotch to see how much of a man you are. Fanatics upset the balance of the universe.

In the sixties my father took our family from California to Greece to enter politics in my grandfather's party. We children and my mother – an impressive brunette born in a working-class suburb of Chicago whose father taught her to work hard, live clean and not complain about the weather – learned to inhabit two worlds. When I told my American grandfather about the evil eye, he washed my mouth with soap because I was speaking nonsense. When I told my Greek grandfather, he spat on my forehead and told me not to look anyone in the eye for twenty-six hours. I read *Batman* in English and *Little Hero* in Greek, a comic about a pint-sized adolescent who was unfailingly cleverer than any German paratrooper. With equal pleasure I wolfed down my Greek grandmother's baklava and my American grandmother's apple pie – a pie which won her first prize in the 1932 Illinois Home Bake Jamboree and was considered by many to be the best pie east of the Mississippi.

Simply because of the chance circumstance that my father and grandfather were politicians, Greeks would hug me, kiss me, lift me up in the air, ask me to marry off their daughters – or marry them myself – and tell me secrets that only their confessor should have heard. In the Greece of the early sixties, they, unlike me, could sense the 'mysterious hum of approaching events' and the rumble of tanks vibrating in the Athenian air. To protect us from the oncoming dictatorship, they gave us icons, they lit candles, burnt frankincense on our steps, sprinkled basil-dipped water on the steps of our porch, or hung metal *tamata* on the fence and spat on our heads to ward off evil.

In April 1967, the night of the coup, a fanatic such as I've already taught you to recognize came to arrest my father. At the age of nine I had an irrepressible need to imitate sounds: the put-put of a *kaiki*, the strangled cry of a donkey, the alarm clock and the sizzle of coffee spilling over the *briki*. I thought he was a thief and I imitated the siren of a police car, to scare him. He was not deterred. When he entered my bedroom he looked at me with his invincible gaze. I felt that if I got too close to him I would be sucked into an empty space. He must be alive because I still see him in my dreams.

That night weakened our family's centrifugal gravity, loosened the orbits. My sister turned inward and grew less talkative, while my older brother blamed himself for his father's arrest and hurled himself into politics like a Minoan dancer. My youngest brother barricaded himself behind a deceptive smile, and I had recurring dreams of being strangled by the fanatic officer. As for my parents, in the ensuing years they exhausted their love for the 'ultimate good' and sacrificed it for the all-absorbing 'struggle' of politics. Politics is an enemy to family, an opposing force. At some point love, no matter how strong, hides and cowers in the corner while politics, hot, naked and sweating, moves in like a Minotaur.

I tasted politics when I was eight years old. That was the first time I saw people swarm down the hills of Achaia, a province in Northern Peloponnesus which was both my grandfather's birthplace and his electoral district. Priests with staffs, shepherds in sheepskin overcoats, children in bare feet and tattered shorts, indestructible old men and ancient stalwarts descended to listen to the 'Old Man of Democracy' give a speech in the square of King George I. Taxi-drivers, pipe-fitters, farmers in their black Sunday suits, long-haired girls of angelic beauty whose poverty had not yet killed their freshness, all coming to hear my grandfather, who had been speaking 'for the people' since 1908 and who, in his mid-seventies, had become the country's greatest orator. In him a century of poverty had found its voice. With him was my father, whose sudden immersion in a Greece divided into first-class and third-class citizens gave his sense of outrage a powerful rawness; compared to other Greek politicians he was young. In the Greece of the sixties his Adlai Stevenson liberalism and rhetoric from the Berkeley free-speech movement was a powerful potion, what Greek youth wanted to hear. Together, the ageing and dignified politician and his pipe-smoking tweed-suited son were an almost unbeatable combination, ultimately silenced by tanks, house arrest and prison.

From them I learned that before any speech the crowd is like a caged lion, pulsing with life, hungry with anticipation. When my grandfather stepped on to the podium and leaned towards the microphone to say his first words, the lion was set loose and roared its freedom. Buildings shook, balconies quivered, and the ancient mountains yielded, for once, to a presence greater than theirs. The crowd's roar rose to the very heavens like a thunderclap, carrying my young unformed soul on its wings.

The strangest thing of all was to hear crowds chant my last name in rhythmic unity. Standing on the balcony with my grandfather and my father after a speech, I sensed how it might feel to lead the trembling multitude, to raise its wrath, to give it the full measure of its power, make it laugh and explode without harm. I too wanted to lift my hands into the sky and send thunder over the microphones and revel in sarcasm and wit.

The world of my childhood was a world of crowds, of speeches and cavalcades, of applause and adulation. I grew up inside these crowds. Sometimes I think they are my real parents. I love them. I want them to shrivel up and die. I want them to leave me alone. I want them to forgive me and praise me, make me great and make me humble.

To know my Greece, don't search for exact dates, don't check newspapers for verification, don't ask others who might have lived these events if these things really happened. Just listen. The sound of the crowd is the sound of my life.

2 *My First Baptism*

My first experience of public life, of strangers looking at me, touching me, waiting for me to produce a word of wisdom happened a few years after our family moved from California to Greece. My father, by then a member of the Greek parliament, sent me to Crete to baptize the daughter of one of his party supporters. I was eight years old. I was expected to please them all but I most wanted to please the baby's mother. After I left Crete, I found her note in my jacket.

Dear Mr Alex,

For us it was a double joy your presence, one, for you are now Maria's godfather, and one, for what you said about poets and politicians. I am not good with words like you and your family but my husband wants our son to become a deputy in the Greek parliament like your father and grandfather, which he can't do because he doesn't study. I want you to find him a job in Athens when he turns eighteen. In my son you will have a loyal civil servant who can help you in your important tasks in the future.

Six months ago my husband stabbed his cousin by accident

as a joke during a festival. The man had accepted a plot of land from my husband and they even shook hands. A month ago the cousin sued my husband. If your father speaks to the judge before the trial begins, maybe the whole thing will end before the families get involved. Have you heard of a Cretan vendetta? It takes many men each year. What will happen if my husband is found guilty? The cousin's limp won't improve with my husband in jail.

Mrs Panagaki, your *koumbara*.

Please, I am married and so forbidden by God to speak against my husband so please know that this is not a stone, this is a piece of paper with a mother's plea.

Manoli, a man hired by my father to look after us children, dropped me off at the port of Piraeus, where I boarded the *King Minos*, a sleek white liner with a blue stripe, the colours of Greece. I slept all the way. The next morning the ragged Cretan mountain range stretched across a vast blue sky. The men on the dock looked like nothing I had ever seen before. They wore black riding boots and khaki pants, headbands with lace tassels across their foreheads, cartridge belts across their chests, and most had thorny beards and bushy eyebrows. When I reached the bottom of the wooden ramp I heard one of them shout, 'He's here! He's here!' They rushed towards me and surrounded me, pressing close. They pinched my cheeks, held my face in both their hands, and patted my head. Their coarse skin smelled of gunpowder and meat. When one moved back another came forward to see and touch me.

He looks like an American!

Does he have his grandfather's voice? He certainly has his nose.

You see what happens when a Greek man marries an American woman? You get this.

Looks just like his mother.

Just like his father.

His grandfather.

I was completely unprepared. I knew little of Greece and could barely speak Greek. I had seen my grandfather give speeches to large crowds from the balcony but I had never faced a crowd alone, even a small one like this.

A man pushed through the group and made some space for me. He was the only one in a suit. He shook my hand and welcomed me to the 'Democratic island of Crete'. This was Mr Panagaki, the father of the baby girl I was to baptize. He looked a little disappointed. I knew he would have preferred my father or, failing that, at least a larger boy, bulkier and more Greek-looking than me. I had blond hair, blue-green eyes, and a freckled face; my skinny knees protruded below my grey shorts. I knew I would have to work doubly hard to make up for my deficiencies. The men pushed close, searching for some proof that I had inherited my progenitor's blood, some evidence that I was blessed. When I shook an old man's hand with as much strength as I could muster, he shouted 'Bravo! Bravo!' as if this were a sign.

Together with the eager, excited men, I stumbled towards the cars. Mr Panagaki sat me beside him in his blue Opel. Worry beads hung from the rear-view mirror, a magnetic Virgin Mary was stuck to the dashboard, and the steering wheel had one of those knobs that allow the driver to swing the wheel with one hand. In an accident those knobs punched into your chest like a piston and were illegal, but this was Crete. Another man sat on my right and four more piled into the back seat. We set off. A cavalcade of cars followed us like we were on the campaign trail. In the car the Cretan dialect seemed incomprehensible, a sibilant shushing of sounds, thick esses, soft tees. The man next to me patted my head and rubbed my face. Mr Panagaki squeezed my leg as if to make sure I was still sitting next to him.

We stopped to let a turtle cross. Mr Panagaki was superstitious about all slow-moving creatures – too close to Satan they were, he said – and on the day of a baptism, the day the godfather banished Satan for ever, it would not do to squash one of his earthly representatives, 'although on any other day . . .' he said, and smiled without finishing his sentence. One of my father's drivers would hunt down cats when I was in the car. 'Got one!' he would say after the sickening thump.

Now we rounded the top of the mountain and began our descent. At the bottom I could see chimney stacks, tiled roofs, white-washed streets and a church belfry. The entire village was waiting for us. Women wiped their hands on their aprons, dusted their clothes, rolled down their sleeves and rushed towards the car. Children grabbed at the door handles. '*O Nonos*! The Godfather!' Men ran alongside us shooting rifles and revolvers in the air. 'If a stray bullet should hit someone,' Mr Panagaki shouted, 'let Hades take him. His time is up!'

The kids wrenched open the door as soon as the car stopped and we tumbled out. A woman squeezed my neck with fingers strong as pliers. '*Vre*, look what's here, the grandson!' Sometimes I was the grandson, other times the son, depending on whether the sympathizer preferred the more moderate politics of my grandfather or the more radical messages of my father. With evident pride of ownership, Mr Panagaki ushered me towards his mansion. Green pails with basil sat on the outside steps. I was pushed up the steps, into the house, past a table laden with sweets that smelled of cloves and cinnamon, and into a living room where a number of wooden chairs lined the walls. The group stared at me and whispered. I wanted to hide. Why couldn't I look more Greek? Was I really Greek? Wasn't it true, as I had told my parents, that I had been switched at birth by some accident at the Kaiser Hospital in San Francisco where I was born and that someone else who should be me was sitting on a swing in Tilden Park, a smug smile on his face?

Mr Panagaki finally rescued me. He took me around the room and introduced me. First the great-grandmother, Kira-Evgenia, who sat knitting; at ninety-five she could still thread a needle better than any of the girls, 'without glasses!' Some girls my age sat in one corner, their heads huddled together, tittering and glancing like spies in my direction. Into their braids they had woven gold ribbons, strips of silk, rows of white shells; the light streaming through the open window glinted off their hair. Then I was introduced to Mr Panagaki's son, Pano, a boy a little older than me. 'Pleased to meet you,' he said, and called me *kyrie*, which means sir. His black-rimmed glasses magnified his eyes. He shook my hand meekly yet the *kyrie* impressed me. He's a real Greek, I thought, who knows how to introduce, shake hands, speak politely, and who won't make any mistakes in grammar.

Grammar. Greek grammar. What a humiliation if I forgot the plural of a verb or used a feminine article for a masculine noun or simply mispronounced a Greek word. I was young enough to believe that my father's political future hung on my syntax, his future and the whole family's honour. These people expected me to speak like my grandfather or father. I recalled the dent in my grandfather's forehead where he had been hit with a pistol butt by Royalists; I recalled the long nose, the grey hair, his low and controlled voice. I heard the roar of the crowd, the sustained hiss for the duration of his speech, like listening to the world through seashells. My grandfather's words came more readily than my father's. 'This is not a gathering! This is an earthquake!' I tried to recall what else he had said. 'While the numbers prosper, the people suffer!' That had a ring to it, but had nothing to do with a baptism and might even be considered an insult. While I was searching for a resounding line, Mr Panagaki showed me my seat and I sat down.

His wife entered the room. Her nose was long and straight and her eyebrows dark. All her power seemed to reside in those brows. How could a woman expose her eyebrows so bluntly? Wasn't it like revealing a bra-strap, a slip, or cleavage? I felt she had penetrated the false protection of my name.

'Eat,' she said. She was balancing a plate on her palm. On it sat a blob of candied orange peel soaked in gooey syrup. In her other hand she held a glass of water. There was no refusing a command from her, even though it seemed unjust that I would have to ingest the peel of an orange when everywhere else in the world they ate the orange and threw away the peel. Like so many other things I was to face in Greece, I would have to swallow it and say I liked it. But this offering was from Mrs Panagaki so I thrust a spoonful into my mouth. It was bitter and stuck in my throat. I noticed her muscles tense when I pushed into the orange peel with my spoon. We were in on this together. I had to eat the orange; she had to hold the plate level and stand there in front of me, like a servant. The rest of them stared at my throat as the bitter-sweet peels went down.

When I was done she hurried out of the room. The members of the clan felt more comfortable now, and started talking to each other. But when Mr Panagaki stood, their voices dropped to whispers. The girls stopped giggling and the great-grandmother rested her needles on her lap. He waited until the room was completely silent.

'Tell us a *mantinada*, Nikita,' he said to his brother, a man with a beard thick as a sponge. From his chair, Nikita cleared his throat and spoke.

> Cretan towns that I adore, with mounts and hills so steep
> You produce professors, who know how to steal the sheep.

The family applauded. Nikita rubbed his beard and smiled. The attention had shifted to him and I clapped hard. Pano was fidgeting in his chair, biting his nails, then rubbed his glasses on his trousers.

'You see,' Mr Panagaki said, 'our Nikita invents them as he speaks. That's the Cretan gift. Tell us one about his grandfather.' Nikita looked up at the ceiling, then at his boots, and then into the centre of the room.

> Workers, farmers, girls and boys, from every town in Crete
> Grant the Old Man a day from your life, a hundred years he'll
>   meet.

They applauded again. They were happy that Nikita had managed to praise my grandfather. I had heard similar sentiments on other occasions. 'Take both my lungs for your breath!' people would shout to my grandfather, or, 'Take a year of my life!' I couldn't imagine the mechanics of such a transfer but it did seem so un-American that it confirmed my distance from these people. Pano looked at the floor. I didn't know why he was so sullen until Nikita spoke.

'I may be good,' he said, 'but my nephew Pano is the real poet. He has the spark, eh, brother?'

Mr Panagaki frowned. 'Pano has work to do for the baptism.'

'Come, come,' said Nikita, 'this is a celebration. Let the boy recite one of his poems. Mr Alex has a trained ear, he comes from a cultured family.'

'No, no, Mr Alex doesn't want to hear such nonsense! Mr Alex is a serious boy, you see he sits straight at the chair, head up, not like my son.'

'Your son's also a man,' Nikita insisted. 'He must learn to speak without fear, especially before guests.' The room grew still as Mr Panagaki paced about, and, except for Kira-Evgenia, who had resumed her knitting, it seemed everybody was watching him.

'OK!' he shouted. 'But after that Pano will sharpen the knives for the lamb. Now speak and be done with, tell us one of your poems.'

Pano squirmed in his chair and looked at me. Did he expect me to do something? He adjusted his glasses, cleared his throat, then stood to attention, like a student delivering his homework in front of the teacher. He spoke in a soft voice, barely audible.

A squirrel had a rose in its cheek
I called him crazy;

He paused. His father was facing the window, holding his hands behind his back and rubbing almonds in their pocked shells with his fingers. Kira-Evgenia drew a fresh bundle of golden wool from somewhere inside her skirts. The rest of us leaned forward on our chairs. Pano stared at me again.

My barber's a mouse, the camel's my preacher,
But still I can't find the way into your heart's pain.

He said this in a wavering voice. His eyes were full of watery expression. I admired him but felt jealous too, not only because everybody was watching but because he was saying things in public that were so different from what I had ever heard before. 'Now, my last poem,' he said, smiling weakly.

A bee sleeps in the thickets of my heart.

That was it, a single line, which ended abruptly. The words echoed in the room. Then I heard a loud sound, like an explosion. Mr Panagaki had cracked an almond. Crack! Another one.

'That's poetry? What kind of poem is that? Fairy-tales women tell their children!' He paced as he spoke. 'Of course Mr Alex doesn't like it,' he said, turning to me. 'He wants poetry, not talking animals, he wants words that rhyme, wants stories of Crete, stories about men like Captain Zapheros who at the age of ninety-eight could still fight the Turks like a wild dog, of Digeni Ksiri who stood at his door, musket in hand, shouting to the enemy, "Come and get it!" or old Koutroulis who, seeing his son dead, picked up his weapons and took his place. Where is our tradition? How come my son doesn't respect our tradition?' His face had turned red and the vein in the middle of his forehead bulged. His neck was puffed up, softening the sharp angles of his chin.

'God gave me a son who speaks of squirrels and camels . . .' He was interrupted by a loud wail as Mrs Panagaki carried in the baby. He threw his hands into the air. 'And now God punishes me with a daughter,' he said, 'a daughter that cries all day and night . . . and a boy who is good only for womanish poems.'

Mrs Panagaki had bowed her head. She needed someone to come to the rescue. I remembered once when someone re- leased a single dove just as my father stepped out on to the balcony to speak. The dove flew towards him like a bullet, then at the last moment veered off to the right and disap- peared into a clear sky. The crowd applauded as if my father had caused a miracle.

I was breathing fast as I walked to the middle of the room.

The walls seemed to expand, the dresses and scarves of the women flooded the room with red and yellow and the girls' hair flamed. My knees seemed as large as two spotlights.

They were all staring at me, waiting for me to speak. What was I doing? Why had I stood? Was it for Mrs Panagaki? Was it because I thought this was what my father's son should do? Or was it that I really did want everybody's eyes upon me after all? All sounds were suppressed, as if I had entered a dream-like place. I saw an image of my grandmother sitting on the light blue sofa of our living room, a cameo pendant pinned to her blouse, her feet barely touching the floor. I remembered what she had once told me about my grandfather.

'I'm jealous of you politicians,' a poet once told my grandfather, 'because you meet so many people.'

'I'm jealous of you poets,' my grandfather replied, 'because you meet so many uncontrollable passions.'

My grandmother's words flowed out of me, in a nervous high-pitched voice. Mr Panagaki stopped pacing. Pano sat back on his seat and folded his arms.

'Good show,' Nikita whispered, rubbing his hands vigorously, 'that'll shut my brother up.' Kyra-Evgenia peered at me. I sensed the girls staring at me, and felt a glimmer of satisfaction. And there, Mrs Panagaki was standing straight again. I think she was smiling.

'Did I miss something? Did the boy finally speak?' Pano's grandfather woke up and everybody laughed. I laughed too, a hard, staccato laugh. I gave thanks to my grandmother, that singular constant of my childhood, a very *comme-il-faut* woman who once wrote to the newspapers to correct them because she was not ninety-four but ninety-six; my grandmother who was my height when I was ten, all of four-foot-eleven, who spoke of the day she met Cavafy, the poet, in Egypt; my grandmother who believed politics was the death of the family.

Carrying the bronze baptismal cauldron, Pano and his father led the way on to the cobbled street. Mrs Panagaki, with the baby in her arms, wore a silver breast plate and a silver dagger through her sash. Her black hair flowed down her shoulders and a stray curl drooped across her left eye. Villagers joined us: men in white boots and baggy breeches, women in silk dresses, aprons, embroidered waistcoats. In front of the church Mr Panagaki shouted at the crowd to go on ahead, pushing them forward with his free hand. 'Inside, get inside! Tell the priest to start blessing the blasted place!'

He reminded me of my father in many ways: serious, running the whole show, clearly the leader in the village, a man who inspired respect and fear from those around him. But he was different. I couldn't imagine myself carrying anything with my father.

The priest, standing in the middle of the church floor, requested the presence of the godfather and the baby. His gold-embroidered mantle glinted as he lifted his arms. I stood behind the cauldron and turned to the pews. I was surrounded by a sea of black beards and headbands, of grizzled faces and moustaches, of women's scarves and headdresses. The girls of the Panagaki clan shifted in their seats and the grandfather leaned his chin on his cane. I felt a peculiar strength, as if I alone deserved to be here. This group was my crowd, they were here for me as much as they were here for the baptism. I remembered how my father used to talk about the size of the crowds at his speeches. Ten thousand in Corinth, he'd tell someone; fifty thousand in Patras; a hundred thousand in Salonica. The number of people was a sign of strength. When I returned to Athens I would tell him, casually, 'I had a hundred in the Church of All Saints.'

Mrs Panagaki brought the baby and stood next to me. The baby, dressed in pink, buried its face into her chest and sniffled. Suddenly I realized that when the ceremony was complete I would be a godfather, a *nonos*. My own godfather was a friend of my father's, spoke four languages, walked with a cane, wore three-piece suits, smoked a pipe, and asked me questions like 'Why is a spoon called a spoon and not a fork?' And I still wasn't old enough to knot a tie.

'Do you reject Satan?' The priest leaned over and pointed to words in a red book.

'I reject him,' I replied, reading the answer. But when he repeated his question, as was the custom, for some reason I shouted the answer, 'I reject him!' The priest stared at me a moment, looked away, and continued the rites. For a third time, he asked me,

'Do you reject Satan?'

'I reject him!' My voice resonated beneath the dome of the small church. How good to cry 'I reject!' to anything that forces you to eat orange peel, stands you in a suit on a

blistering day while a few feet away tourists lie on the beach
and cool off in the blue Mediterranean; anything that forces
you to smile while a toothless old lady suffocates you with
kisses; anything that forces you to nod your head while an old
man with a bilious wart growing from his nose brings his face
close to yours and tells you an interminable story about your
grandfather; anything that forces you to lift your arms and
begin a recitation: People of Crete! People of the Aegean!
People of Greece! You are my sovereign, chase me into the
villages of Manesi, Toskes, Velimachi, Alepochori, Aghia
Marina, Kalentzi, chase me into the Erymanthean mountains,
into Mount Olympus, into the seas of Argos and Nafplion,
into the olive trees of Kalamata and Lesbos, into the volcanic
land of Limnos, chase me up to the borders of Bulgaria and
Albania, send me into the Ionian sea, chase me into the only
privacy this country allows, the toilet, preferably the simple,
hole-in-the-ground affair, the Cyclopean eye that stares at
your nether parts, chase me until, cowed and hunched, I descend into my English-speaking conscious, until I'm autistic to
all things Greek.

I heard the crowd shifting in the seats. Who said I couldn't
shout? I was the godfather, no? I was in charge.

'Do you believe in God?'

'I believe!'

Finally the priest closed his red book. He dipped a sprig of
basil and a crucifix into the cauldron and sprinkled me with
water. The altar boy took my candle and draped a towel across
my chest like a bib. Suddenly I was holding the naked baby
while Mrs Panagaki and the priest rubbed olive oil over her

body, from head to toe. The baby kicked and punched the air, and squirmed in my hands. I didn't feel strong enough to hold her. What kind of a godfather was I that I couldn't even hold the child in my arms? I summoned all my strength and lifted the baby over the lip of the cauldron. The priest touched her forehead and then clapped his hand violently over her mouth and nostrils and forced me to plunge her all the way under, until her head disappeared beneath the basil-blessed water. When I brought the baby up she gasped for breath. I heard the priest saying, 'I christen you Maria, servant of the lord . . .'

The men and women laughed and shouted her name. 'Maria!' I stared at the baby's naked body, dripping water, slippery from olive oil. Mrs Panagaki stooped over me and covered my hands with hers. Together we plunged the baby back into the holy water, this time leaving her head high. Her grip was sure. The smell of incense engulfed me and the thick embroidery of her dress rubbed against my cheek. We lifted the gleaming body high above the cauldron. Water dripped on to my arms and face.

Down the baby went for the third and final time. I relaxed my grip to let Mrs Panagaki carry the full weight and she squeezed my hands hard, the way I hoped she would. I wanted to stay there, a prisoner in her warmth, her hands on mine, her body enveloping me in laurel and olive oil. When we lifted the baby up high the two snakes on her ring seemed to be twisting and slithering as the oily water flowed from it.

'Long life to Maria!' The crowd chanted.

'*Ze-tow* Kosta and Eleni!'

'Long life to Alex! Long life to his grandfather!' I clutched the cauldron for support. A tuft of hair floated in the yellow-spotted water.

And then there was the celebration afterwards, the rows of skewered lambs, a lyre and a singer, and the acrobatic *pentozali* dance, where men leap into the air, their boots flashing in the sun. Mrs Panagaki led the women in a dance, twirling her scarf. I drank two glasses of *raki* and promptly fell asleep beneath a pine tree. The next thing I knew I was on the ship back to Piraeus, gripping the rail. A forest of hands was waving at me. I lifted my arms into the air and showed them my palms, without bending the wrist. This was the way my grandfather greeted a crowd.

The ship started to pull out. Father and son ambled along the quay. I imagined they were laughing, because though I couldn't hear anything over the din of the engines, I did see the brightness on their faces. There was something calm and gentle in their manner, the way the father's arm hung loosely around Pano's shoulder, the slowness of their gait. Gone was the father's stern austerity, gone the son's obsequiousness. Again they were doing something together, something I couldn't imagine doing with my father. Had Mr Panagaki forgiven him his poetry?

Away from the island, the air grew cool and thick with salt. I drew my jacket close. The sharp corner of an envelope jabbed against my chest. Something from her? Holding my breath I read her letter eagerly, expecting her to say something terribly important, to tell me what a fine godfather I was, to tell me I was truly my father's son, or maybe something else, something I didn't dare think.

Instead, she was asking me for favours.

I stuffed the note into my pocket, returned to my cabin and curled up in my bunk bed. The throb of the engines carrying me through the dark Aegean sounded like the drawn-out roar of a crowd. I replayed my moments of glory. I saw myself standing in front of the clan, reciting my short speech. I recalled the praise from Nikita, the son's look of gratitude, the shine in the girls' eyes, the rows of faces in the church. Soon I grew tired and tried to sleep, but neither the small pillow nor my hands over my ears were able to make the roar and the faces disappear.

3   The Greek Tongue

When Manoli, a loyal follower from my grandfather's birth-place, moved into our house to take care of us children he brought with him the smells of the village, tales from the mountains of Erymanthos and a joy for life that made us glow. He dazzled us with the feats of someone called Saki, who wore pants cut above the knees, danced naked on water from melted snow and whose voice made the blossoms bloom. He told us the white-washed houses of his village were so bright that from a distance it seemed a piece of sun had fallen there. The dark spots on the moon were caused by all the children over the centuries who'd been throwing stones at it at night. He held under our noses different herbs and with our eyes closed it was as if we were inhaling bits of Peloponnesus.

In the evenings we would gather on the kitchen verandah in our old house in Palio Psyhiko and listen to his stories. Hector chewed his T-shirt and left wrinkled wet spots all over it, while Lydia braided and unbraided her hair, I scratched the scabs on my knees, and Jason blew his hair out of his eyes by pushing his lips forward like an imitation Neanderthal.

My favourite story was the one where Manoli once saw a

large number of angels descend from the peaks and fly into the tavern where he was sipping wine. Their wings were butterfly-coloured. Two angels with exposed breasts sat on his knees and stroked his face, while the tallest one perched on the edge of the table, swung her shining gold-coloured legs and sent light-beams into the room with her broad smile. The rest of them peeled grapes, sliced watermelons, and poured wine into his glass from the diamond rings on their fingers, combed his hair with an invisible comb and massaged his feet. Each angel danced a belly-dance for him while the others clapped with their wings. Finally they flew away into the sunset like giant moths, sprinkling the air behind them with a porphyritic glitter-dust.

This, according to Manoli, was the closest anyone would ever get to paradise. Jason and I agreed that this was a much better version of heaven than anything our grandmother had told us.

His breath sometimes smelled of garlic and retsina. He wore shabby pants and old shoes and loaves of bread jutted out from his jacket pocket. Owing to his bowed legs, when he walked he tottered like a building. When he was young he'd moved to Piraeus and run a pet shop, but he abandoned that when all the animals escaped after an earthquake; he tried selling yoghurt from the village but when that too didn't work he took over as doorman in the apartment complex in Tambouria where he had been living.

The part I liked best about Manoli was that he was an adult who talked to us as if we were important. 'Dear children', he called us, or 'kind audience'. 'Listen, my dear children,' he might begin. 'I read in the newspaper today that Pope Paul VI has sent the remains of Saint Andreas from the Vatican to Patras, with a ceremony overseen by 2,500 cardinals and bishops, all of them silent as the still sea. Think about it. The Church takes saints and spreads them around the whole country, so that now Saint So-and-So has a finger in Trikala, a leg in Tinos, a veil in Corfu, and a face in Athens; the moment a saint dies, he's torn to pieces by the Church. Ha! I'd become an atheist if God would let me!'

Often he would take us into his arms, rub our heads, ask us if we preferred history to maths, and whisper something about the properties of garlic for the heart, the use of a rabbit's foot in curing us of chicken pox, and why eating a frog's head helps increase the male population. He took us to see *Geisha Boy* with Jerry Lewis and *The Fall of the Roman Empire* with Sophia Loren and Omar Sharif; he had bought us each our own tube of Kolynos toothpaste, Greece's first domestically produced toothpaste; for five drachmas he bought us a small palm-sized calendar to record the saints' days; and he informed us proudly of the invention of the Wankel engine, which was based on moving triangular pistons and possessed magical properties of propulsion.

After years of governesses who were either unable to keep us under control or who beat us with rulers or knitting needles (the Greeks usually adhere to the spare-the-rod-and-spoil-the-child philosophy), it was a relief to be in the company of an adult who didn't dare raise a hand against us. What's more, he knew how to get us to stop fighting with each other. If I chased Hector after he'd turned one of my comic-books into toilet paper, or if Jason knocked our heads together for playing one of his Jefferson Airplane LPs, Manoli would intervene, speak calmly and say, 'The children of your father don't fight,' or 'Save your energies for the enemy.' He told us we could hit each other as much as we wanted but first we had to ask his permission – he knew that by the time we registered a formal complaint the initial urge would have been dissipated and we usually forgot why we wanted to hit each other in the first place.

But what was really different about Manoli was that he talked aloud. He would read the newspaper aloud, speak to invisible friends from his village, and once spoke for an hour to Kree-kree, his long-dead pet parrot. This wasn't a sign of insanity or senility, he claimed. Words didn't exist if they were not spoken and heard by at least one ear, whether that ear belonged to a human or to a donkey. What were you to do with silent words? Not for him reading books or newspapers with your eyes alone. A book was to be read aloud, shouted aloud, enjoyed by everybody. That brought the book to life, you could hear the characters talk, smell what they smelled, taste what they tasted. That's what democracy is about, after all, he said: the public person who doesn't hide like an eel in the depths but swims like a salmon in the surf. 'How can anybody think without actually saying the words?'

This habit was not restricted to the kitchen or the back verandah. He told us that when he worked in the yoghurt shop he would comment on the customers coming in and this would get him into trouble. 'Boy, that man looks fat as a whale,' he might say before he knew it, or, 'I wonder if her husband likes her moustache.' That was why his business never succeeded and why the pet shop was indeed the best place for a man like him, since pets never got upset by what he said. 'One day,' he said, shaking his head in profound sadness, 'I will also leave this home, for talking too much.'

Once he took Hector and me to the fruit and vegetable market next to the church of Saint Sophia to buy water-melons. When we got there, he went up to a stall, held up a watermelon, rapped it with his knuckles, and, in front of the astonished vendor, started to say things like, 'I wonder if this is worth two drachmas per kilo or if the vendor is trying to rob us? This seems like a rotten watermelon and I think I should move to another stall. I'll bet anything this man is a Royalist. Just look at those narrow, gypsy-like eyes, those thick eye-brows and his dark, dark skin, like a foreigner, this man isn't a Greek, he's probably a Bulgarian.' At which point the vendor picked up a knife and shouted, 'Who'd you say's a Bulgarian?' We shuffled off and Manoli apologized and told us to tug at his jacket if he started talking too much.

One afternoon we heard his loud metallic voice coming from the back yard. It sounded more like a speech than the monologues and one-person dialogues we were accustomed to. His voice rose and fell, paused for imaginary applause, and ceased so abruptly you could hear the punctuation. Had he gathered old women and priests and passers-by in our back yard? No. He was standing alone on the balcony, speaking to the bushes, the eucalyptus trees and the gravel, plus a stray cat stretching itself lazily in the hot sun. 'The king is the people's enemy!' Manoli shook his fists at an aeroplane that interrupted him as it droned lazily over Athens. 'The Old Man of Democracy says that when there are people lacking a house and bread, none has the right to be rich!' I closed my eyes and was convinced he really was speaking to a crowd but when I opened them again all I saw were the bushes and the pebbles and the trees. The cat was gone. Lydia stared at him and then looked down to work off a small stubborn stain of nail polish. Hector laughed and Jason twirled his index finger next to his temple.

I don't know if my parents knew about these habits of his because, though he was loud and determined with us children and the visitors that gathered in the kitchen, in my parents' presence his strength and talkativeness fizzled out. Then he would grow quiet, his eyes would shine and he seemed to shrink, as if he dared only to look at my parents from a lower place. In the early evening when my father sometimes came home to change clothes before going to Parliament, Manoli would smile and his eyes would shine for hours afterwards.

That summer, while temperatures rose to above ninety degrees and the pine-cones crackled from the heat, the Royalists declared a truce in the war between them and my grandfather's supporters, to celebrate the young king's marriage. It was Manoli's bad luck that though our family was considered strongly anti-monarchist, my father's public office required his attendance at the wedding. For me and for my siblings, the occasion was one of excitement, not only at the prospect of seeing royalty, but because for once the whole family was at home, preparing.

We polished our shoes, showered, combed our hair, sniffed each other's heads, and let our mother inspect ears and finger-nails. The place smelled of nail-polish remover because Lydia changed her mind, from raspberry red to vanilla orange to sky blue.

By early afternoon we were ready. My father was dressed in a tuxedo with a tail, a starched white shirt and a red ribbon across his chest. He held a top hat in his hand and he stood at the top of the stairway and bowed for us with a slight smile and sparkling eyes. I think he knew that he looked like some-thing from another age. My mother wore a bottle-green dress and elbow-length gloves.

But if the process made me happy, it had the opposite effect on Manoli. For him our presence at the wedding was akin to national betrayal, treachery, punishable by execution. He paced around our rooms with his hands behind his back. 'How could he?' he said of my father. 'The king! And you mean to tell me he will make more royal children? When will we put an end to this race? How can this family, of all families in Greece, be attending his wedding?' He paced nervously around the house, slammed the door of the kitchen. He told Hector and me not to make our shoes too shiny, they would only get dirty again out in the streets of Athens.

None the less, despite Manoli's entreaties, we embarked for Athens in separate cars. The streets of downtown Athens were lined with people. Flowers garlanded the telephone poles and flags from nations around the world hung from balconies. From the Church of the Metropolis to the Temple of Saint Dionysus bells were ringing. When we arrived we were shown to a dais erected especially for the government officials and their families, and we took our seats.

Marching past us were so many swords, horse-whips and cuirasses that there would have been enough to start a war. Horses snorted and rose on their haunches like in a battle-scene from the last century. Dukes, barons, counts, all related to each other, sat in gleaming carriages with canopies folded back like ruffled satin. The men wore tight uniforms with medals pinned to their chests and the women wore diamond tiaras, flowing scarves and gold bracelets.

Hector kept saying things like, 'Alex, look over there. Cool! Look at that!' Manoli cursed under his breath. 'May his black soul rest in Hades,' he said as each member of the royalty passed by. With every ah and ooh of the crowd Manoli felt it his duty to respond. 'Come, now, a princess? More like a wench. Look at that one with a moustache. Who does he think he is? Bismarck? Why look! It's Metternich!'

Among the brilliant princesses with their bewitching jewels and the tall aristocrats with their sparkling medals I searched eagerly for the Greek royalty. Thrilled and impatient, I waited for them just as I waited for the Greek team to appear in front of the other teams in the opening ceremony of the Olympic games. But when they drew close I was disap-pointed. Our royal family fitted into a single carriage, drawn by four magnificent horses whose magnificence tried vali-antly but vainly to make up for the gap in our history. Greece had no dukes, counts, barons, or knights. It had a king and a queen-mother, and now a queen. That was it.

The king was handsome enough, that was for sure, with a

full head of sleeked-back hair and an impressive nose. He was standing up in the carriage, staring straight ahead. He reminded me of a little boy with a fresh hair cut who's waiting at the corner for the school bus. When they passed right in front of us Manoli's cursing grew so loud that heads turned. In a loud whisper my father demanded that Manoli be silent but Manoli continued. Only when my grandfather turned his statuesque head in Manoli's direction and drew his white eyebrows together did Manoli shrink back into his seat and keep his mouth shut. From that moment on he didn't make a sound, not even when the new queen went by, her blonde hair flaming like a halo in the hot Athenian sun, not even when she turned towards our section and my grandfather tipped his head to her in acknowledgement, like a father giving his blessing to his daughter.

On the way back home Manoli stared at us with a sad, owl-like gaze, and shook his head. I felt sorry for Manoli. He seemed genuinely crushed.

'The king wasn't so bad,' I whispered to him timidly.

Lydia nodded her head and added, 'Maybe you can become friends.'

Manoli looked at us as if we were crazy and then leaned his head against the window.

That night I was awakened by Manoli's loud voice. I shook Jason but he told me he was too tired for games so I left him alone. Hector was too young to wake and my sister Lydia didn't like being disturbed in the middle of the night. I sneaked out alone. The marble stairway cooled my feet. With my body safely behind Manoli's door I thrust my face in front of the crack and peered in. Two peeled figs sat on a wicker chair like fat pashas. An empty glass lay on the floor and next to it an empty bottle of retsina, the cheap kind that comes with a metal bottle-cap and not a cork. Manoli paced the room and clenched and unclenched his fists. In his boxer shorts his bowed legs formed an arch. He stopped pacing, grew still and seemed to listen for sounds like a dog sensing a fox. I pulled away from the crack.

Suddenly I heard him shout, 'Mouth! O dear mouth, why can't you please shut up? Must you betray me again and again?' When I looked again he'd retrieved a mirror and was holding it up to his face. 'You made the Old Man angry! You should be ashamed! You know what I'll do? I'll glue you shut, do you hear? I'll pray to god to seal your lips for ever.'

Manoli glanced towards the door and I moved back into the darkness once more. I felt sure he knew I was there. My heart was beating so hard I thought he would hear it; my chest rose and fell and I held my breath. When he resumed talking I sucked in the air.

'Remember when a man chased me because I said that his eight-year-old daughter would make a fine whore one day? I only meant to say that she was beautiful. And now this job, the job of my life, taking care of his grandchildren, being in his family, this, too, is one more dream you've ruined.'

I dug my nails into my palms.

'This time I must end my sins,' he added in a cold voice, 'once and for ever.' He retrieved a small penknife from his drawer, the tourist kind with the map of Crete on it, and started shouting 'I'll cut you out, I swear, if you don't shut up, I'll just cut you out!' Then he grabbed his tongue and brought the knife close to it. His tongue slipped out of his grip and flipped and flopped like a fish. Finally he caught it and held it hard between his fingers. He continued to talk, but instead of words he made soft gurgling incomprehensible noises. My head buzzed and my stomach felt queasy. The objects in his room suddenly grew startlingly clear, his ragged loaf of bread, his shirt hanging from the wooden back of the chair, his big toes which pointed slightly inward, as if he'd grown up wearing shoes that were too tight. The knife touched his tongue. I imagined his tongue dropping to the floor, the short piece of red flesh quivering like a snake, and then I imagined him turning to me with his bloodied mouth, emitting an awful gargling sound. He was no longer the Manoli who told me stories.

Shaking, trying to keep my teeth from chattering, I pushed open the door and stood there in front of him. There was a white glint in his eyes but I don't think he saw me. I jumped up and down, trying to reach his field of vision.

'Manoli!' I shouted. 'Do you hear me?' He seemed helpless, as if someone else was holding the knife. I tugged his T-shirt hard and when that failed to shake him, I put both hands against his waist and pushed. That did it. He tumbled a few feet away, released his tongue in an effort to keep his balance and the knife fell to the floor with a clatter. His sweaty feet, lifting off the wooden floor, made a sound like paper being torn.

That's when he saw me. He dropped to his knees, wrapped

his arms around my skinny legs and pressed his head against my chest. My T-shirt grew damp from his hot breath. I saw a large dark birthmark on his head, hiding beneath the thinning hair. In a muffled voice, because he was speaking into my stomach, he said his soul was troubled, that he still loved his brother who had died in the civil war, and finally that seeing the king and my grandfather together was too much for him. His jaw worked against my stomach, up and down, up and down, and I felt his chin next to my belly-button. Could a man give off so much heat? He was suffocating me.

I pressed as hard as I could against his shoulders, like a genie trying to extricate itself from a bottle. Finally he released me and sat on his bed. The springs squeaked. His hands, resting on his knees, looked like empty gloves.

I turned around very slowly and, sensing his eyes staring at my back, I grew aware of my pyjama shorts and the skinniness of my legs and wondered how I must look from the back. He could keep me in this room if he really wanted to, with the strength in his large eyes alone. Hadn't his sister, the *mantissa*, told him how to cast the evil eye? I dashed up the marble stairs, taking the steps two by two. I raced past Hector's room, banged my knee on the handle of a closet, cursed but didn't pause, and then I jumped into my bed and covered myself with the sheets. I listened to Jason breathing and stared out of the window into a sky glittering with stars, impatient for the night to end and the sun to come out.

I fell asleep thinking that if I had been a bit older, I might have been able to walk in, put my arm around his shoulder and tell him that neither my grandfather or father were emperors whose every whim and wish, like modern-day Caligulas, had to be obeyed. I would have told him that politics is not something for which you slice off your tongue. But I was a child and he was the adult, and he was supposed to explain the world to me and not the other way around.

Next day Manoli packed up the same battered grey suitcase with which he'd arrived, wore a white hat we'd never seen him wear, and mumbled something to my mother about matters concerning the health of his dear sister who lived in Macedonia. We gathered at the front of our house to see him off. Hector pointed at Manoli's white hat, Lydia held a hand up to protect her face from the sun, and Jason looked everywhere but at Manoli, glancing to the left or the right to hide his disappointment. Manoli kissed each one of us goodbye, like a soldier going off to war.

We never saw him again, nor do I know what happened to him. I imagine him haranguing villagers about the king and I see barefooted children trailing after him to hear about his angels sitting on his knees, peeling grapes and combing his hair before flying off into the sun.

The last thing I remember was how he wobbled down the narrow street, tottering like a building, slapping his hat against his legs to free it of dust, and then, as he rounded the corner, clearing his throat loudly as if preparing to speak to the air and tell one more story, maybe this time about a man who wanted to cut off his tongue and a little boy who believed he saved him.

4 *Day of Secrets*

My father believed that it took a lot more than elementary
school and my grandmother's lessons to bring our Greek up
to scratch so in the summer of 1966 he sent his four children
to different parts of Greece to get to know the customs of the
people. My older brother, Jason, went to the island of Skopellos, my sister Lydia and my younger brother Hector ended up
in camp in Pilio, and I was sent to the southern mountains of
Peloponnesus, to stay with Mr Veneti, the uncle of Yorgo, my
father's political secretary.

That's how I found myself, one fine day in July, running
up the hills of Rozena with two dark-faced kids with crew-
cuts whose legs were an atlas of bruises and half-healed scrapes.
'This is Spiraki, Yango's son,' Mr Veneti had told me when he
introduced me to a skinny boy with wide eyes and a long face.
'Born in one shot, *mia rixia*, ptou! Just like that, didn't give his
mother Annoula any problem, skinny as a *samiamidi* and just as
quick.' The other boy, Taki, 'a well-fed good-for-nothing',
was much larger than I was and had a shadow of a moustache.
'I don't care what time you return,' Mr Veneti had said the
first day, 'as long as it's before midnight.'

It was almost dark when, panting and sweating, we came to a sheep-pen like the kind you see on the road to Patras. The roof had collapsed and the rectangular stones were piled up against one of the walls and the place smelled of manure and hay. Using twigs, thick branches and leaves, Taki and Spiraki quickly built a fire to push away the dark. This was the first time I'd seen kids make a fire. Not only that, but they had their own matches.

While the light flickered and cast shadows on our faces, they showed me their small collection, which they drew forth from a worn wooden box tucked between two stones: a tiny wedge-shaped snakeskull, three dark brown coins from the fields, and a tattered postcard of a half-naked woman. We held the picture close to the fire and stared. She was a little fat but her breasts pointed straight up and something stirred near my groin. In return I leaned over and let them tear the label – 'Made in USA' – from the neck of my T-shirt, which they added to their hoard of treasures.

I let them try on my shoes, which were sturdier and thicker than theirs. Spiraki clumped around in them like they were too big and quickly took them off. They asked me what my house in Athens looked like. I had never had to describe it before and I found that I couldn't remember the colours of the walls, the height of the ceilings, or the amount of property we owned. They wanted to know what the traffic lights looked like, if everybody had a car in America, at what age you could get your licence, and they wanted a list of all the different kinds of cars I had ever been in. Taki was fascinated by the inside of the government cars with the silver grilles and cross-hair backlights. Did they go faster than Cadillacs? Were the windows bullet-proof? Did we carry machine-guns in the back seats? I knew the answer to that one and I was sure I impressed them.

Two small thick-bodied lizards – *samiamidia* – crept up to the fire like soldiers moving on their stomachs. The lizards hopped into the air and brought down a small white moth. They caught two more, then Taki pushed them away with a burning stick, stood up and with the same stick pointed to a thicket of lights on the mountainside – 'That's Rozena,' he said. 'The next two, higher up, are called Zarouklayka and Ovries.' He looked like a teacher in a planetarium.

I stood and pointed to the moon. It was missing a piece.

'When it's full,' Spiraki said in almost a whisper, 'the Day of Secrets begins.'

The Day of Secrets. It sent a chill down my back. At that moment I wouldn't trade Greece for all the hot-dogs and Mars Bars in the world. They told me that every August the thirteenth the village gathered to tell each other their secrets – the men with the men, the women with the women, and the kids with the kids. On this day people said whatever they wanted to say to each other. The women could speak about their husbands without fear of God and they could gossip about their neighbours without worrying about the evil eye. The men could call each other names, get angry, and swear.

'What kind of secrets?' I asked.

Spiraki and Taki looked at each other.

'It's late,' Taki said. He threw away the stick and it left a bright trail as it tumbled through the air. Then we kicked dirt over the embers.

The next morning I was woken up by cocks crowing. When I went into the living room, Mr Veneti was sitting on his creaky wooden chair. He was a tall, imposing man with an Adam's apple that moved when he spoke and large, veiny hands. He was also considered to be the village wise man, the *sophos*. People stared at his bookshelf through the window and when kids passed by parents slapped their heads and brought them in to see how many books an educated person had to read to become educated. A man with so much knowledge in one room – this had made Rozena famous. Mr Veneti was also famous for serving visitors a bitter concoction of unknown ingredients that Taki had warned me not to touch. It smelled harsh – like he'd boiled twigs of oregano.

I was so excited by last night's adventures that I would have gladly downed the bitterest drink and said thank you on top of it. I hoped Mr Veneti didn't notice that I was barefoot. I wanted to roughen up my feet, I wanted my hands to grow hard and callused like Taki's and my hair to grow blond and dry from the sun. I stared out of the window at the hills and couldn't wait for the afternoon to arrive. I wanted to ask Mr Veneti about the Day of Secrets but I held back and instead I wandered around the living room and without much thought retrieved a large book from the shelf. The inside cover was an abstract purple and yellow design, rather like the psychedelic patterns on some of my album covers.

'Wow! Published in 1845!'

'Yes,' he answered and rose to his full height. He reminded me of doctor Zervos, who used to give me injections in my bottom. 'I own over three hundred old books, some dating from the Revolution.' His large hands swept upwards and downwards like wings. Lined up along the thick stone walls and running all the way to the ceiling were rows of hardback books, most of them black or burgundy, serious and adult-like, just like in my grandfather's study. They filled the home with a cool darkness.

'Have you read them all?' I asked.

'Nope,' he replied, shaking his head. He stared at my bare toes but didn't say anything. 'Some books are too big between the covers. Some are so thin they're not worth their wisdom. Then there're the books that don't like you and you don't want to hold.' I looked at him blankly. 'Just kidding,' he said and stretched out a long hand to muss up my hair. 'What's the use of books if they're not read?' Then he nodded as if agreeing with some invisible person just off to my right. I nodded too.

Mr Veneti didn't seem to be concerned by my comings and goings, as long as I ate lunch (usually mashed potatoes and meat) and dinner (vegetables with meat). But he was touchy about his books. He didn't like me to stare in his direction while he read or try to discover what book he was reading – in short he didn't like me to pry. I soon discovered that he was working on the same book – Aristotle's *Poetics* – reading it over and over, from front to back, at least once a day.

Passing by him one day, I saw that he was working on

chapter five. I brought out my own book and every now and then peered at him. It wasn't the speed with which he turned his pages that impressed me – I took this to be a sign of age and experience – it was his calm demeanour, the almost religious quiet that overtook him from the moment he sat down until the moment he got up. I must have been staring pretty hard because he turned towards me as if he'd felt my gaze.

'What's wrong with you,' he said loudly, and then he slammed the book shut.

'Do you know about the Day of Secrets?' I blurted out.

'*Panagia mou!*' Holy Mary! He came towards me with quick, nervous movements and I took a step back. His eyes were bright with anger. 'A celebration of fools. Is that the only thing those useless boys have to tell you about this village? I call it the day of gossip. It gives the villagers something to talk about for the rest of the year. That's because nobody in this village reads.'

'Do you have any secrets?' I asked.

'Who doesn't? But such things are for women and illiterates. You want to learn? Do what I do – read.'

That night, just before bedtime, I sneaked into the living room, took his book and placed the bookmark at the beginning of chapter two. Next morning, while we sat in his small garden, he opened it and read from there. I guessed he'd read it so many times it didn't matter where he began. But another night I did something sneakier: I located a book of approximately the same weight, size and colour, and switched it with the *Poetics*. This one he picked up and started reading without any visible reaction. I decided that either he had read his books so many times that he'd learned them by heart or that he knew what I was up to and was playing games with me.

Some mornings, while we were both reading, I would hear what sounded like a ponderous flapping of wings – it was Mr Veneti flipping slowly through the pages. That was what happened when you read for years and years, I thought, you took in a page at a single glance. I figured that at my rate, by the time I reached his age I would have polished off less than 900,000 pages.

A sort of routine developed. Each morning I would sit in the living room and read, then Taki and Spiraki would come by and we would spend the rest of the day in the hills. We played *gourouna*, *melissa*, *mountzouri*, and *pentovola*. I learned that the rooster, the *kokoros*, went *keekee-reekee-koo* and the owl, the *kookoovaya*, went *koo-koo-vow*. We made statues from lard and dirt, cleaned old donkey saddles, heated watermelon seeds until they burst into flames and burned insects. I gave them two *Batman* comic-books and one *Superman*, and in return got indefinite loan of the nude woman postcard.

To turn crying into laughter, the boys taught me to sing 'Cries, cries, he laughs, seven farts he blasts.' When Spiraki lost a tooth, we tied his tooth to a string and hung it from the roof of a house.

> Dear crow, take my teeth and give me one of steel
> So I can chew on metal, and grind the village meal.

Taki stole a cigarette from his father and we smoked it up in the abandoned sheep-pen, sucking in hard, and when the cigarette was nearly done we threw it to the ground, huddled over the burning butt and drank in the smell until the air carried away the last of it. My lungs burned all night and as penitence the next morning I downed the bitter drink. It tasted like the juice from boiled turnips. 'Some things taste awful,' Mr Veneti told me with a wry smile as he watched my face pucker up, 'but remember that when you're finished with them, the whole world looks a lot better.'

Another day Taki led us past the sheep-pen and to the other side of the mountain. He turned left and right at certain pine trees as if it made a difference which path we took. We soon reached a sort of plateau with a sprinkling of bushes. Taki lifted his head, clapped his hands, and shouted 'Birds! Birds! Come out!' And out they came. Two birds were felled with their slingshots. A third stood, hobbled about like a tiny penguin and fell over.

'Stop!' I shouted. 'Cut it out!' They looked at me in amazement.

'Why?' Taki said, puffing up like overheated milk. 'They're only birds.' He took aim at another bird and suddenly I jumped up and took a flying tackle at him. Spiraki and Taki were on me and began kicking and shouting. The earth smelled of oregano and manure.

'Butterboy! Butterboy!' I managed to pull Taki's feet from under him and he landed on his head with a terrible thunk and lay there motionless. Spiraki and I stopped beating each other and attended to Taki but Taki was only pretending. He opened his eyes and got me in such a stranglehold I thought I would faint. Spiraki kicked me in my behind, like in the comics. Then, having defeated me, they let me go. My lip was numb, my shoulder ached and more than anything I wanted a slingshot to sling stones at their heads. I hated them for being so strange, so Greek. I kept my head low, picked burrs from my socks and shirt, and tended to a scrape on my elbow. Spiraki licked a cut on his finger. Taki dusted his shorts and checked his bare sole for something, then spat into his palms, rubbed them together and wiped his face.

'Don't tell Veneti,' Spiraki said first, plucking a burr from his shorts.

'This is how tough you are?' My bloated lip made me dizzy because it wouldn't disappear from the corner of my eye.

'Listen,' Taki said. 'We can talk this over.'

'Too late.'

Taki threw a stone in the air, watched it rise and fall and then spoke again. 'We'll take you to the day of secrets. You'll hear everything.'

This was what I wanted to hear more than anything else but I wondered whether the exchange Taki was offering me was actually such a fair bargain. Except for Manos, who collected money to buy a generator from Athens but lost it all in a game of backgammon, and Anneli, the widow, who looked a little like the woman on the postcard, life in the village seemed calm and ordinary.

'Tell me a few secrets from last year's celebration.'

Spiraki spoke now, so fast his words ran together. He was eager to strike the deal.

Secret: after every birth the village midwife cut the first little boy she met with a razor blade so he too could see how it felt to bleed like a woman.

Secret: Katerina, Marko's wife, rubbed rabbit legs between her legs each night because she couldn't have babies.

Secret: Mrs Konioti poured evaporated Carnation milk on her breast for her baby because she didn't have any milk herself.

'OK,' I replied indifferently, though I was now fully convinced. I put out my hand. 'Deal.' We shook. 'And no more *butterboy*!' They nodded in agreement.

While walking back to the village, Taki put his arm around my shoulder and said, 'You'll have to tell your own secret now,' a satisfied grin on his face. 'It's the only way to take part in the Day of Secrets.'

'Won't you tell me about the Day of Secrets?' I asked Mr Veneti the next morning.

'*Pedi mou!* Again? You want secrets? Look in your books!'

He plunked himself into his chair and cracked open a book. There was something awkward and forced the way he sat down like that. I suspected he took up that position each morning just to make sure he could be seen from the window. Diligently and without further word I bowed my head and stared at the page which now looked like a mass of indecipherable black etchings.

The following day I sat down again and opened my book, *A Boy Counts the Stars*, at page 189, which began, 'Life was a dark beast come to devour dreams.' But very soon I abandoned all pretence of reading and gave myself up to my real task – reconstructing the secrets I'd heard.

I saw a woman like the one in the postcard removing her blouse and pouring Carnation milk over her breasts; in the neighbouring bed another woman slithered around and rubbed a rabbit leg between her legs. These were such great secrets. How would I compete? None of the secrets I'd come up with seemed likely to impress the boys. A man on a motorcycle had stopped in front of my sister, unzipped his fly and showed her his thing. A ship's captain had tickled my older brother between his legs until a bodyguard threw the captain into the sea. My father didn't want my mother on the balcony when he spoke because her presence made him nervous.

As for the village I had learned a few things, but nothing that resembled a genuine secret. I'd seen a little boy squat behind Mr Veneti's house to go to the toilet and suddenly a flock of chickens raced up and pecked at his white butt. Kloukias the shepherd swore all the time and they said that's why he didn't enter church, because he was afraid the saint of Rozena would kick him out. Konstantis, a retired merchant-seaman, rode his donkey from dawn until dusk, dreaming of his days on the seas; there was Kyria-Angela who had baptized fourteen children and the fifteenth, the first one to be named after her, drowned in the well; and there was light-shadowed – *alafro-iskiotos* – who spat out food 'for the devils who were hungry'. They said he was touched by angels but I had only heard about him, never actually seen him.

★

The Day of Secrets Mr Veneti told me to dress formally. I hadn't slept that night. I had tossed and turned in bed and when I woke up my mind was filled with these hazy images of birds and books and books and birds and other things that made no sense.

'I don't believe in these things,' he said on our way out, 'but I respect the traditions.'

In the village square a group of musicians played a clarinet, a tambourine, and sang as loud as they could. The boys were dressed in black shorts and short-sleeved white shirts, their hair plastered back, and the girls, who looked much older than their age, wore embroidered white blouses and plastic pins in their hair. The large maple tree in the middle of the street had been trimmed and its trunk painted white. Some men filled metal pitchers from three wooden barrels and others brought great chunks of steaming roast lamb to the rows and rows of tables.

We sat next to Spiraki's family. His mother was skinny and ate little but his father ate huge hunks with his hands. He spoke, chewed and drank wine all at the same time and, though he was Spiraki's father, he reminded me of Taki, who sat at another table and kept looking over in our direction. People got up from their tables to shake my hand and ask me things like whether my grandfather would bring a telephone and electricity to each and every house. They reminded me how lucky I was to be living with Mr Veneti, the most educated man around.

When we had finished eating, the mayor announced that it was time for the Day of Secrets to begin and told the men and women where to go. We kids were free to go anywhere we wanted.

Spiraki pinched me. Taki ran up to me. My heart beat faster than the rhythm of the Kalamatiano music but when I got up Mr Veneti gripped my arm, pulled me close and showed me his bony face.

'There are secrets and there are secrets,' he said. 'Do you understand?' I didn't know what he meant so I nodded my head. 'Go,' he said. 'But be careful.' I followed Spiraki and Taki, and along with some other boys we ran up into the hills and came to a place where the weeds grew high.

Taki said that for the Day of Secrets to begin he had to make a small sacrifice. He looked at me for approval, then drew his slingshot and very quickly felled a single sparrow. We sat in a circle surrounded by tall weeds that reached as high as our heads. Taki picked up the bird and twisted its head until we heard a slight snap. 'To make sure,' he said and looked at me, his eyes shining brightly.

I didn't let him see how I felt. With the bird lying in the middle we joined hands, shouted '*Zdoh! Zdoh! Zdoh!*' and threw our hands up into the air, like players charging up for a game of soccer. The wind rustled through the blades and cooled our faces.

'I go first,' he said, 'since I caught the bird.' His eyes were bright. 'Makri's baby arrived only six months into the marriage. It was fat and round and sprig-haired and looked more like the *koumbaros*, their best man!' The boys clapped his back and Taki perked up like a peacock preening.

Taki handed the dead bird to the boy next to him.

'Dounis is a wild man,' he said. 'I looked through the key-hole and saw him dancing naked. He was singing those crazy melodies!'

He handed the bird to the next boy.

'Kir-Kosta the slaughterer forces his wife to drink bull's blood once a month so that his next child will be a boy! Malamo had a seventh child, but it too was a girl. Her husband stepped on the baby's neck on purpose and strangled it at birth. And now he doesn't even allow a female cat into the house!'

I tried to think hard about what I would tell them. What, what? Another boy was talking: 'Old man Koutroulis is doing it with Panagitsa, his thirteen-year-old niece.' I recalled the chicken coops behind Mr Veneti's house, and the chickens pecking at the little boy as he squatted in the long grass with his trousers round his ankles. But this was no secret, at least not to these boys who seemed to know so much about everybody in the village.

I felt this growing pressure on my chest. My breathing grew short. Spiraki held the bird gently, with respect, as if it were still alive. 'For confession,' Spiraki began, 'instead of touching his stole to Elenaki's forehead, the priest asked her to kneel under his robes. And you know what?' The boys leaned forward but I was barely listening. 'He wasn't wearing anything underneath!' This was the best secret so far.

And then they all turned to look at me. I felt my face grow hot and stared at the tangled mess of feathers suddenly placed on my knee by Spiraki. The bird was so light I was certain that if I threw it into the sky the wind would carry it away. At first I didn't dare touch it and then I began rubbing its head as if it was still alive. The tiny beak was smooth, like a fingernail.

'C'mon, Alex,' Spiraki said, 'the secret! Surely you have greater secrets than us?'

The wind picked up and chilled my back and suddenly the bits and pieces of last night's dream came together. I saw myself walking through a great gloomy library but when I looked more carefully I saw that the shelves were full of dead birds, each one lying inert, a title etched into the beak. Mr Veneti climbed a ladder, retrieved a bird as big as an albatross, swung it over his shoulder, descended the ladder, took a seat, then laid the bird on his lap, spread open its wings and with a sudden sinister glance my way, started to read.

That's when I realized that wise old Veneti couldn't read. That the people coming by to look at him through the window were being fooled. The whole village was being fooled. That he turned the pages over and over as if he was reading but had no idea how fast to turn them or how slowly. That was a secret worth telling. I stared at the bird in my lap and looked up at the boys. Spiraki's eyes were wide, like when I first met him. Taki pretended to be stretching his slingshot but I could tell he was listening. The other boys were perfectly still.

'Tell us,' Taki said. In his eyes I saw a hungry, sneaky look.

I looked at the bird. Its tiny head leaned to one side and I thought of Mr Veneti. My words had power. I understood how just saying something might change 'the existing order of things', though at that age I couldn't phrase it quite like that, but I had an inkling, an understanding, that this village, for all its craziness, had its own rules. One rule was that everyone had a secret.

Including me.

'When my father becomes prime minister,' I said, 'he's going to shorten the school week by one day. No more school on Saturdays!' At this the kids shouted and clapped me on the back and Spiraki actually kissed me. 'But don't tell anybody in case the adults find out and get him to change it back again!'

When we were done we crossed ourselves and with great solemnity stood and threw the bird down a ravine. Its tiny body fell noiselessly.

I left the boys in the village square. They were huddled around a wine barrel and competing to see who could drink the most. I returned to Mr Veneti's house, with its rusty-orange and bright red bougainvillaeas hanging over the weathered shutters. Mr Veneti was pottering around the kitchen and moments after I had come in he offered me a cup of hot chocolate and a great slice of *halva*. We sat down at the wooden table.

'Learn any great secrets?'

I nodded my head. 'One boy said that Mrs Varela sprinkled chilli pepper on her kid's mouth because he told lies, and now his teeth are rotten.'

He laughed. 'Is that so? And how does he know?' He shook his head. 'Did you tell any great secrets?'

'Nothing important,' I replied, squeezing the cup with both hands. My face grew hot. 'I told them a lie.'

'Ha!' He stood and clapped his hands. 'Isn't that the way it is? Indeed. They should call it the Day of Lies.' His hands fluttered. 'That's what I always say. Lies! All lies!'

In the remaining days at Rozena I taught Spiraki how to make three different kinds of fisherman's knots – I'd learned plenty of them in the Boy Scouts – so he could impress Taki. Mr Veneti no longer felt compelled to spend all his time with his books on his lap and instead he took long walks in the hills or sipped coffee in the village *kafeneion*. I was dying to tell someone my secret and I didn't want to wait until my return to Athens. I had to tell someone, but who?

The night before my departure I slipped the postcard of the half-naked woman into the beginning of chapter one of Aristotle's book. On the back of the card I wrote, 'Mr Veneti: I know you can't read. Signed – Alex, August 13, 1966.'

5 *First Son*

Hector believed that jellyfish were so-called not because of their transparent body but because you could actually spread them over bread and butter, and to prove it, one summer on a beach in Skopellos, he retrieved a light blue jellyfish, laid it out on a piece of driftwood, chopped it into pieces with a blunt knife, and, while it shimmered at the tip of a bamboo stick, offered it to us to eat, slice of bread included. None of us took him seriously so he himself nibbled a tiny bit of it. 'See,' he proclaimed, 'see!' He said it tasted like fatty sea-water.

The beach stopped at the foot of a hill. Sea-water and fresh-water fish gathered at the spot where a small stream poured into the sea. Splashing and shouting, we tried to force the fish into invading each other's territory but they wouldn't cross over. They merely scattered, re-grouped and stared at each other from their separate worlds. Hector said it was a good way to clean the salt off your body. Jason said the fish reminded him of the Greek *kafeneia*, the village-square coffee shops frequented only by supporters of the same political party.

One day Jason and I, armed with masks and snorkels, decided to look for octopus. Weeds, tiny fish and small stones swayed and drifted back and forth with the heaving rhythm of the sea. Soon enough I came across the remains of an octopus meal: a crab-pincer, the empty hull of a sea-urchin and a tiny fish skeleton, picked clean from head to tail like in cartoons with cats.

'Octopus!' I shouted when I spotted it. 'Octopus!' I plunged my head beneath the surface to keep track of it. Its head grew bulbous and large, then suddenly emptied into something flaccid and limp, like a balloon that has lost its air. One moment it was an ugly spotted green, the next it was a brilliant orange-blue. The two black spots at the base of its bald head were its eyes, evil and sinister.

I watched Jason dive down, body wiggling and legs kicking, arms pointed in front of him. He swam along the floor, looked around and made an angry questioning gesture to me as if it was my fault the octopus had suddenly gone invisible. When he came up for air he had blue lips and pink lines across his forehead from the pressure of the rubber mask.

'It's gone!'

We swam slowly back to shore. 'Don't tell anybody we saw it.' You either had the goods or you didn't, that was the way he was. We sat on the beach, listened to stones plop as we threw them into the water and let the salt stretch the skin across our backs.

'You know what I want to be when I grow up?' I said. Jason threw another stone. 'An underwater archaeologist. If Mom will buy the scuba equipment.'

'Isn't that expensive?'

'Yeah. Like a car.'

'Mom won't.'

'Maybe when I'm older she will. In the meantime I'll search in shallow places where no one else has ever looked. I might find sunken ships, ancient Greek coins, necklaces, or rings. I'll give you half of whatever I find.'

'You will?'

'Wouldn't you?'

'Well, I'd give Dad and Mom some too. And then there's the people that work around the house, like Elvira, the gardener, and Vasili the kiosk-man.'

'Yeah, but after that will anything be left for us?' I already saw my sunken treasure spent making sure nobody could say a word against us.

'You shouldn't care about us or yourself and things like that. Don't you see what Dad's doing?'

'Is the king that bad?'

'He's against the people, don't you know anything?'

'Yeah, but what has he done?'

'It's enough that he's a king. You'll understand when you grow up.'

'What do you want to be when you grow up?' I asked, but Jason had stood up and was hurling stones. 'One, two, three –' he was counting the number of skips along the water, '– five, six, seven!' Farther out the breeze rippled the surface so it looked like bicycle treads.

'Wanna dredge up a sea-worm?' I patted my hair. It was thick with salt.

Jason smiled and shook his head. 'We'll get into trouble.'

Last time we caught a sea-worm we lodged it inside the

grape-vines that shaded the beach-side taverna and, at the appropriate moment, just when the food was being served, Hector, Jason and I pierced it with sharpened bamboo sticks. It spurted out streams of water like a miniature fire-engine and when it was cleansed of water it shot a gooey white liquid into the air and over our food. Like melted cheese. The bill had come to one solid spanking and no dinner.

'So you are the two sons!' A loud voice startled me and I looked up to see a tall shepherd standing over us. He spread out an old blanket and sat down. 'I don't like sand,' he explained. Though he was old, and this I could tell from the rawness of the skin on his face and his large bony hands, he moved quickly and efficiently. From somewhere inside his clothes he retrieved an onion, which he promptly and cheerfully popped into his cavernous mouth. He rolled it to the back of his mouth where it protruded from his cheek, and with one hand on his jaw and the other on his head, pushed until the onion cracked.

'Only two teeth left,' he said. 'Now, let me ask you. Which one of you will follow in your father's footsteps?'

I waited.

'Who is the wild one, the leader, who is the leader?' The shepherd stood, shook out his blanket with an annoyed expression and sat down again.

'Jason is!' I cried. Jason was still throwing stones. 'He's never afraid of anything. He once caught an octopus with his bare hands. The tentacles were all over him, suckers big as mushrooms.' I looked at Jason but he said nothing. 'When he grows up,' I continued, 'he'll take all the king's treasures, the coins, the necklaces and the rings, and hand them out to the Greek people. He's not afraid of anything.'

'The first son, that's the way it should be,' the shepherd said and clapped Jason on the back. Jason remained still, expressionless, regal. Yes, Jason was the one, of that there was no doubt. Why then did I hate him a little at the very moment of his success? The shepherd lifted his head back and bit into another onion. Then he patted my head.

'Let me tell you about your grandfather.' With a silent groan – everybody talked to us about him – I lay down and started to cover my body with sand. Jason leaned back on his elbows and flicked small stones into the water.

'When your *pappou* returned to Erymanthos when he had become famous, all the villagers avoided him.' The shepherd paused and spat. He seemed to be thinking, or maybe that was just the way he spoke. 'When he walked towards the coffee-house, three men turned their backs on him; when he went up the hill, two others skittered away like goats. He knocked on many doors, but they were all closed. And this after he had built two thousand schools around the country, and one in his very own village.' I had never heard this story. By now both legs and my groin were solidly ensconced in sand.

'Finally he found an old man who was too incapacitated to move. Your grandfather drew up a chair and sat next to him. "Why is everybody avoiding me in my own village?" he asked. "Because you have done them so much good." "And is that a reason to avoid me?" "Yes. How will they ever pay you back? They are poor. They don't even have thirty lepta to buy you a coffee."'

The shepherd spat out bits of onion skin and with a stick ruined the even heap over my stomach. When I looked up, he winked.

'Now, let me show you how to make those stones skip like crazy.' Jason rubbed the sand off his arms and they both stood. 'You have to choose the really flat ones.'

I watched them walk along the beach and bend down for stones. I kicked free the blanket of sand on my legs, then squatted and proceeded to make a pile out of coloured shells, stones like emeralds, and other nearly invisible treasures. Jason was the first son, of course, and that made him special, but my anger at him soon vanished in the cool afternoon breeze.

6 Red Hearts and Winged Turtles

From the isthmus of Corinth on, the road was packed with buses, cars, tractors and horse-drawn carts, all heading to-wards Patras. Yet my sister Lydia saw none of this. During the four-hour trip along the national road not once did she wave at the other passengers, not once did she shout out of the window, 'Down with the king!' or, 'Long live democracy!' the way I did. We had a duty, I believed, to wave to these people; after all, they were coming to see our grandfather give a speech in the city of Patras so the least we could do was show them that we appreciated their support – even if they didn't know us.

When I saw one car garlanded with carnations, a quivering floral garden, its roof plastered with posters of my grandfather, I found a legitimate excuse to reach back, grab my sister's shoulder and say, 'Look at that car!' But she shook free and retreated to the far end of the seat, behind our bland-faced driver, where I couldn't get hold of her. She brought a painted egg close to her face, turning the delicate white sphere this way and that and staring at it with religious awe. I wanted to smash it against the window. It was a gift from her boyfriend.

She no longer read the same books I did, no longer rode her bicycle with me, no longer went to the movies with me on Saturdays. She had just turned fourteen. She thought she was the smartest, cutest thing this side of the planet earth. Right now she was wearing lipstick, a jade necklace, an amethyst ring from my grandmother and two earrings from the Navajo Indians in Reno where we spent a summer before moving to Greece. Also, she drenched herself with patchouli, giving off an odour stronger than insect repellent.

Memos, the object of her love, was a gangly sixteen-year-old with sideburns and longish hair, who — when not draining eggs of their yoke for my sister — copied Rilke's poetry into her notebooks and gave her exotic things, like the dried-up shell of a sea-urchin, a small chunk of obsidian from the island of Milos, and the unabridged version of *Erotocretos*, 'The Cretan Lover', a 366-page ballad of rhyming love couplets. On her desk in her room she kept a piece of drift-wood from the beaches of Sounion on which he'd carved three words and when doing her homework she would sud-denly close her eyes and pass her fingers over the words. 'My Braille love,' I heard her say once.

Only when we reached the outskirts of Patras in the late afternoon did she return the egg to its bright red box, cocoon-ing it in cotton which she would replenish regularly from a bagful she'd brought for the occasion, like changing sheets. Neither the fishing boats loaded with people nor the pre-war motorcycles with side-buggies full of extended families could distract her. When we slowed down to enter the city, she leaned against the door and pressed her forehead to the window with such an expression of sadness that she looked like a princess on the way to execution, taking a final look at the unsuspecting peasants through the window of a moving train.

In the lobby of the Hotel Majestic a group of people from Patras swarmed over us, hugged us violently and pinched us. One pulled the flesh of my neck so hard I nearly cried. When I grew older I vowed one of the things I would do would be to squeeze some adult's cheek with tremendous force, make his eyes water, and then I'd smile and say, 'Aren't you cute! Aren't you the sweet one!' People beware, they'd say when they saw me strolling up to them, here comes the Pinchking, the King of Pinches, his fingers are the strongest and most unrelenting pliers ever to nab flesh.

But there was one man who impressed me because he stood to one side and didn't touch us. Though he looked as poor and ill-dressed as the rest of them, there was something different about him. Maybe it was his tar-black hair, which was sleeked back and oiled down, or the dark circles below his eyes which made him look as if he had been up all night. A bright yellow tie hung loosely from his neck, making his face seem even darker.

He leaned towards my sister but didn't touch her. I realized I'd seen someone with the same dark glimmer in his eyes, as if he was staring inwards. The previous year a man had tried to run me over while I was standing in front of a coin store on Stadiou street in Athens. I was saved by the strong hands of my father's beautiful secretary, Titina, who saw the car heading towards me and lifted me into the air at the last moment.

Racing by, the driver turned to look at me with eyes dark like burnished marble. He was my first fanatic.

In the hotel bedroom I was bursting to tell my sister about him. She couldn't ignore him the way she ignored the crowds gathering in the streets of Patras. Here was something that might show her there was more to life than her egg. But I wanted to find the right time to tell her. I sat on the bed and punched the pillow like I'd seen in a movie. Soon the pillow looked like a pear because all the stuffing had collected at the bottom.

'Alex, enough.' I rolled along the bed and sat on the edge and tied a few tassels that hung from the bedcover into knots.

'Can I tell you something?'

She gathered up her skirt and sat down in front of the bedroom mirror. 'What is it?' She spilled items from her make-up bag. In a calm, convincing voice I told her about the man in the hotel lobby. She glanced at me from the mirror and quickly looked away. My voice rising, I tried to explain about the fixity of his gaze, the way his whole body angled towards her in yearning. I told her he looked like the man who had tried to run me over and that maybe he, too, was one of those fanatics who hated our family.

'Yeah, right.'

I'd failed. I didn't know what it would take to convince her that in a country like Greece, dangers lurked around every corner. She lifted the lid of the red box. I bounced off the bed and stood next to her, my chin a few inches above her shoulder. In the mirror I saw my tousled hair and a small gap where I had cut away a chunk of hair to get rid of some chewing gum Hector had stuck there. Between her index finger and her thumb she now held her cosmos. She scrutinized the surface – perhaps for signs that his love might have diminished since she last looked. In the mirror her face and the egg looked strangely similar.

'God, it's *kataplyctic*,' she said. In our own version of Greek and English this meant 'incredible'. She closed her eyes. 'It's *so* light, this thing called love.' She sighed and held the egg close to her heart. With great care she wrapped the egg in a pair of stockings and placed it on top of a pile of clothes from her pink suitcase. The egg looked like something from the sea caught in a net and I wished it would sink back into the churning depths.

I jumped back on to the bed and used it as a trampoline, bouncing up and down and touching the rough surface of the stucco ceiling.

'Enough! Time to prepare for tonight.'

Instantly I jumped off the bed, raced to the bathroom, showered, dressed in my too-large black pants and hand-me-down white shirt and, looking like a clownish midget waiter, I sat in front of the bedroom mirror. Lydia stood behind me and dried my hair with a towel, rubbing so hard and fast that my head buzzed, then she squeezed some Brylcreem into her palm and rubbed it into my hair. Her nails raked my skull. Heaven. She parted my hair on the left side, then the right, then down the middle, then no parting at all, each time standing back and narrowing her eyes along the edge of the comb like she was aiming a gun. 'Definitely not down the middle, you look like Little Lord Fauntleroy.' Finally she settled for a parting on the right and when she was done she brought her head down and squeezed her cheek against mine. In the mirror our faces were two bright orbs pressed together, smooth from the small measure of time distilled there.

She pulled away and my cheek grew cold. The grooming process was over, much too soon. I sat there a while longer, staring at myself in the mirror, enjoying the tiny bolts of electricity still racing around beneath my skin.

'Lydia, you think I'll be bald when I grow up? Like Dad?' I hid my hairline with my hand.

'Yeah, maybe. It runs in the family.'

I walked around with my hand against my forehead and jumped up and down, saying, 'Bald dald, hey, look! I'm bald.'

Shouts from outside propelled us to the balcony. In the streets large groups of people carried banners on which were written slogans about democracy and my grandfather and the king. Lydia put her arms around me and I could have stayed like that until the morning except that I saw the man with the yellow tie sauntering casually through the crowd as if he were roller-skating, taking long strides, criss-crossing the street, dodging bodies, at one point going against the flow, his face disappearing behind a banner and then coming up again at another point in the crowd.

'Lydia!' I shouted. 'Look, it's the man!'

He stopped for a moment as if he had heard me. He moved his head slowly to the left and right. I moved away from the edge of the balcony. 'He's looking for us,' I whispered.

'Don't be such a little boy,' my sister said as the man disappeared among the crowd.

'Maybe he'll cast the evil eye over us.'

'Evil, my eye.' Lydia returned to the bedroom and sat in front of the mirror. She drew the pencil-liner through her eyebrows and checked her right and left profile, licked her lips and kissed a piece of toilet paper. The lipstick was deep violet, and her lips looked as if they'd been stuck to an iceberg.

I bounced on the bed. 'A boy was born with a hoof for a foot because someone had cast the evil eye on his mother,' I told her.

'You're gonna ruin your hair.'

I stood next to her again and we looked at each other in the mirror. 'Will you just listen?' I made one final effort. 'A man sliced his thumb with his own breadknife because his wife stared at him; and the maid's husband fell down in the middle of the street and she had to bring someone to undo the spell so he could get up again. Remember Gilda's puppies? I stared at three of them and all three died.'

She loved puppies. 'Leave me alone.'

When we went to the balcony again, an enormous sun was setting over Patras and an extraordinary freshness radiated from the sea. Phantom ships of wind rippled along its surface. Fishing boats continued to arrive. The port was now transformed into a carnival of light.

'Don't you look the little man,' my mother said when she saw me. She touched my stiff hair. 'My, my.' She adjusted my bow-tie and did up my belt another notch. I was so thin my stomach puckered inwards and I could feel the belt's hard bite around my hips. My skull was sore. Victoria, Mother's friend from New York, leaned over and kissed us, then wiped her lipstick off our cheeks with a moistened finger. She wore a red chiffon dress that stuck to her stockings and she had to stop twice to unstick them as we walked down the stairs. Whenever I could, I stared at Victoria and I think she knew this because when she kissed me she held her lips to my face a little longer than most adults and caressed my neck. In the lobby my mother and Victoria were the tallest around. They were like two brilliant fires. My grandfather called them his American Beauties.

My mother told our driver she didn't want to go by car because she wished to be close to the people. We stepped into the street and entered the flow of bodies. I could already hear the throb of the crowd that had gathered in the square. A distant roar, a scattering of slogans, isolated cries. The beast was forming. The sight of the crowd, as I knew from my grandfather's speeches in Athens, was more thrilling than any amusement park, scarier than any thunderstorm, more violent than any war movie.

More and more bodies cascaded into the streets until we were slowed down to a shuffle. I was soon inside a thicket of legs; at eye level were belt buckles, blouses pulled free, shirt-tails hanging loose, jackets held over arms. Wrapped inside this tight cocoon of humanity I felt safe. Purposely I leaned against the person behind me, sank into his burly form. The edge of his woollen jacket rubbed against my face. Two hands held my shoulders and pushed me gently forward; I leaned sideways, my ear against someone's button, and was instantly righted. The rules of touch and not-touch were different inside a crowd. There was no gravity here, the laws of physics no longer applied. I stood on one leg like a flamingo, knowing I couldn't fall. I closed my eyes and leaned into Victoria. She assumed someone had knocked me over and made no fuss. She smelled of jasmine and I inhaled as much of her as I could.

'Alex, grow up!' My sister knew what I was up to.

My mother grabbed our hands and we sneaked into a narrow passageway, opened a dusty door and walked up three flights of wooden stairs. At the top a man with the harried, nervous movements of a grocer who has too many customers in his shop smiled nervously when he saw us and led us to a balcony. Spread out below us was a shimmering mass of humanity, thousands and thousands of people, a huge beating heart. From the sidestreets and alleys, from the main roads and boulevards, more were coming.

And they were shouting our name.

Victoria shook her hands as if she'd burned her fingers and stood on her tiptoes like a little girl. My mother leaned forward, cupped her hands over her mouth and shouted something and then with a smile she lifted her hands because none of us could hear a thing.

From a balcony to our right a man in a black suit tapped the microphone with his finger and then announced in colourless Greek my grandfather's impending appearance. His words echoed through the square like a drum roll. A hushed silence followed the drum roll as thousands of souls drew in their breath and waited expectantly. Into this void strode my grandfather, tall, white-haired, carrying a rose in his hand.

The crowd let loose a roar that shook the buildings in the square and unfurled itself like a great flag into the sky above. My grandfather raised his hands and nodded his head to them as if to say that he best of all understood their blurred vocabulary. He waited patiently for the storm to pass and only then did he venture to speak. 'People of Patras!' he said, leaning forwards into the microphone. The roar that followed his first words drowned him out so he paused before trying to launch once more into his speech.

I yelled into this human hurricane and it was as if I were making no sounds at all. I shouted slogans and then shouted words like *egg* and *eleemosynary* and *shell* and *bald* and made yawping sounds. I yelled in Greek and in English. I felt free and anonymous. The crowd absorbed my cries into its own. Not even my sister – squashed against me, hands folded across her chest – noticed that I was shouting inanities.

That's when I saw the man with the yellow tie. He was hanging from one of the scaffolds, not too far from where my grandfather hovered above the crowd. Sitting on a metal rung he swung his legs back and forth as if this were a picnic.

'Look!' I nudged Lydia. She deigned to cast her eyes in that direction. 'It's the fanatic,' I yelled into her ear, 'and he's not clapping!' She lifted her shoulders, indifferent and unhearing.

Now I no longer heard the crowd nor did I listen closely to my grandfather speaking about the crucifixion of democracy and the road to Golgotha, about Judas and Beelzebub and the thirty gold coins paid for a colleague's conscience. For me there were now only two people in the square. A man that didn't applaud and a little boy who watched his strange behaviour.

After the speech we went to a taverna in the port. We were joined by Zahos, tall and wiry, who slaughtered calves and collected sea shells; Dounis, a Caravaggio-faced repairman who hummed church hymns and sang my grandfather's speeches; Kyr-Antonis, a heavy, bow-legged villager who lugged a generator from home to home in a small cart and re-charged the batteries of old radios; Yorgo, from my grandfather's village, with his large wet eyes that seemed to be perpetually on the verge of tears; Fat-Mary and Antiope, midwives who cleaned our fish. Lydia, dieting, ate only the bland boiled zucchini.

My mother was saying something to my grandfather, who was leaning forward to hear better, but already people were lined up behind him, patting him on the back, kissing him and congratulating him on the speech. He had kissed me earlier and I could still smell the lemon cologne. In his embrace I felt as safe as if I were in the crowd. When he bent down to hug me I noticed, as I always did, the dent in his forehead, the souvenir from a fight with Royalists in the 1920s when he was the governor of the island of Lesbos.

When the people around him had gone, Zahos said that the crowd was so large that it might scare the king into doing something bad. My grandfather had no time to respond.

'Beautiful granddaughter,' Yorgo interrupted, turning to my sister. 'She's already a woman. I wonder whose heart she'll break.'

'Nobody's,' our grandfather replied, and held her chin in his hand. 'She'll marry the first man she meets so she won't have to break his heart.' My sister pulled away. She hadn't forgiven him for pouring a glass of wine over her head last week at lunch. 'For good luck,' he'd said. The wine had darkened her dress and matted her hair. She had pushed back her chair and run out like an insulted lover. 'That's your grandfather's way of showing how happy he is with you,' my father had told her on the drive home.

'Lydia doesn't care about politics,' I said loudly, 'because she's in love.' She dropped her fork – spattering her sleeve with freckles of olive oil – and pinched my leg. 'All she can think of is this dumb egg she carries around.'

Suddenly my sister stood and spoke in her best adult voice: 'The king won't buy any of this democracy stuff.' All heads turned in her direction. 'Greeks have one of everything,' Lydia continued, encouraged by the silence at the table, 'one king, one country, yes – but only one drachma, only one shoe, and only one sock.' She must have read this somewhere and was repeating it as if it was her own. She sat down and looked at me with a smug smile.

'Who said girls can't become politicians?' My grandfather removed the rose from his lapel and handed it gallantly to my sister. She kissed him on his cheek. What a trickster. She, interested only in Memos, pretending she knew about politics. She fooled them all. I raked my nails along the plastic tablecloth, hoping the sound would make her cringe.

Someone said something about a fight that had broken out on the wharf after the speech.

'A fanatic stared at us this morning,' I interrupted. My statement was honoured with a respectful silence and by people looking around. But when I mentioned the man's yellow tie, Zahos laughed.

'That's Trellantonis,' he said. 'He's crazy. He does the opposite of what he sees. If someone's laughing, he cries; if someone's shouting, he grows quiet.'

I kept my head low and concentrated on picking out the bones from the red mullet.

'He thinks he's the prime minister of Greece,' Zahos added.

'He's not the only one,' my grandfather said, lifting his glass. Everybody laughed. Glasses clinked.

My sister poked my arm. 'Alex thinks that Trellantonis cast the evil eye over me,' she said loudly. Fat-Mary knocked on wood and did something with the salt shaker. My grandfather pulled her over and spat air on her forehead three times.

'Gross,' Lydia said, but in a whisper.

Back in the room my sister sat against a propped-up pillow and lay the egg in her lap.

'You see,' I said, 'even *Pappou* believes in the evil eye.'

'Well, I don't. Neither does Memos. Those are Greek superstitions. I'm an American.'

'Half an American. But that doesn't mean we can't be hexed.'

'Hext vext!' She undid the pin that held up her hair and shook her head so her hair tumbled this way and that. 'Why did you have to tell everybody about the eggs? What's it to you?'

'It's dumb, that's all.'

'You're just jealous.'

We didn't say anything for a while. The crowd's after-roar hissed in my ears. I repeated our last name over and over, like a tune stuck in my head.

'Did you see the waiter? The one with the long sideburns and the black hair? Didn't he look like Memos?'

'He looked like an idiot.'

'Yeah? Well, you're too young to understand about love.'

'I'm the one that knows about the evil eye. It'll be too late for you when you find out.'

She rested the egg on the bed and took out her diary. I flicked the lamp on and off.

'Stop it,' she said, 'I want to read something I wrote.' She flipped through the pages. 'Listen. "Love; the reduction of the universe to a single being. The expansion of a single being into God." That's a quote from Victor Hugo, the great French author.'

'I'm in love with Victoria.' I rubbed my bare feet against the thick rug.

'You don't know what love is. And you don't know that rugs are dirty.'

'Are you going to get married to Memos?' I sat next to her.

'Maybe. Why not?'

'You're too young.'

'In Greece sometimes they marry at fourteen. I'm fourteen.'

Egg in hand, she turned off the lights and we went out to sit on the balcony. I curled my toes on the cold marble. The sea glittered from the kerosene lamps of the dozens of fishing boats leaving the harbour. A huge moon rose in the sky. The hollow sound of footsteps echoed below as scattered groups, remnants of the enormous crowd, walked through the streets.

'It's a night for moondreams,' Lydia said. Her fine hair danced in the breeze. She held the egg up to the pale moon. I sat cross-legged on the chair and hugged myself.

'Here, Alex, you try.' I pretended not to want it at first, kept my arms folded in front of me, but I couldn't hold out. Slowly, deliberately, she laid the egg in my palm. I had never held it before.

'You're right,' I said. 'It's so light, as if it's not there.'

Turning it slowly I saw what Memos had painted on the shell: a green heart, two pairs of silver wings, my sister's name in yellow — the first and last letter towering over the middle ones — a blue star, a turtle with wings, and a scorpion-like thing riding a chariot. The breeze picked up. I shivered. My sister put her arm around me. We breathed in the night.

Neither of us could imagine that on a night not so different to this one, an officer of the Greek military who'd come to arrest my father would throw Lydia out of bed and slam her against the wall. Neither of us could imagine that soldiers would stab her mattress with their lances, trample on her jewellery, and crush her twelve painted eggs, while she lay on the floor inert, a mass of long hair and limbs. Nor could I imagine that later the same night I would crawl along the floor of her room and gather up as many broken shells as I could.

Sitting on the balcony of the Hotel Majestic, where the planets of politics, of poverty and protest, of kings and prime ministers and fanatics and soldiers were invisible, I asked her, 'You really think I'll go bald?'

'No *dummkopf*, that was just a joke.'

I held the egg up to the moon.

'*Kataplyctic*,' she whispered, and scratched my head with her nails.

7   *Athenian Runner*

One Saturday in September 1965 Jason and I stood at the front of a large crowd, at the edge of the main runway of Athens airport. Heat rose from the wavering asphalt and the air smelled of tar and aeroplane exhaust. Jason fanned himself with a newspaper – I stood right behind him to receive any stray wind he might send my way – and Yorgo, who had brought us here, wiped his forehead and tugged at his tie, looked at his watch and muttered that he would faint if my father's flight didn't arrive soon.

Earlier that week a heat wave had descended on Athens such that not even my grandmother had seen before. You had to lick chocolate bars off the silver foil and eat ice-cream instantly. Brutus, the neighbourhood dog, gave up chasing the stray cats and sat glumly in the shade with his head between his paws. At night you sweated in bed while ambulances raced through the streets, carrying the heat-stricken. But this hadn't prevented the riots.

The front pages of the newspapers showed pictures of policemen clubbing students demonstrating against the king and dragging them into armoured vans. For me the police were like the Spartan soldiers, and in my ancient history class I always sided with the Athenians, mainly because I was certain I would have been thrown off the Kaian cliffs for having failed the Spartan requirement for discipline and normality. Omonia Square and Panepistimiou Street were barricaded by burned buses and gutted cars, doors, chunks of marble and raw pieces of pavement. One picture showed a ramshackle pile topped with an upside-down billiard table, legs sticking up into the air like a skinny woman.

At the airport people passed around bottles of water and Jason and I took a few sips before passing the bottle on to the next person. I liked this sharing, it gave me the sense that we were doing something special, that these were times in which nobody could care about germs or things like that.

From a distance, racing down the tarmac, four or five buses headed our way. In the haze the buses appeared soft, as if they were bent in the middle. Brakes squealing, they halted right in front of us and disgorged dozens of policemen. An officer gave some orders and the police walked lazily around and took up position. Jason and I were pushed from behind; Yorgo pushed back and shouted, '*Ela!* You want to trample us or what!'

A few policemen stared blankly in our direction to see what the commotion was about but kept their distance. They appeared harmless enough and they didn't remind me of Spartan soldiers one bit. They wiped their foreheads, leaned on one leg, and fanned themselves with their caps.

'Fascists!' someone shouted, but the cry was not taken up

by others in the crowd. A single 'Down with the king!' echoed, strangely out of place in the dry air. Suddenly a hand pointed to the sky. 'He's coming! Look!' For a while I could see nothing. Then there were more shouts. 'There it is!' Everybody, including the policemen, lifted their heads and watched the glinting plane shimmer in the heat and float lazily in our direction. An officer barked orders and the police spread out and tramped around in various formations, holding their clubs. 'It was a mistake for me to bring you out here,' Yorgo said. 'Wrong, plain wrong.'

The aeroplane grew large, hovered above the runway, then, with a jolting screech, touched the earth and taxied to a halt. The engines were turned off but the four propellors continued to spin in silence. The policemen now formed a tight line in front of us and linked their arms – but there was little heart in it. The heat deprived them of any discipline and eroded their spit and spiffle.

A square-jawed steward made his appearance at the top of the stairway and then he stood aside and made way for my father, who stepped out, loosened his tie, and paused to take in the situation. I knew these were his favourite moments, finding himself in front of the crowd, going from airborne SAS passenger to Athenian leader. He smiled as if he hadn't noticed the police, held up his hat, and waved. The crowd roared his name and shuffled forward. A surge of energy seemed to lift me into the air. Another bus drove right up in front of us and unloaded about thirty more policemen.

All the propellors had stopped spinning save one, which now came to a slow and mesmerizing halt and suddenly I recalled a thin electrician who lodged a cigarette behind his ear while he repaired my grandmother's monster fan. 'Tell your father to be careful or the king's men will arrest him.' Now my father was walking right into their hands – their lackadaisical manners and slow, unthreatening ways were simply a trick to fool us. Nobody, not even Yorgo, understood.

I pushed past Jason, ducked under the police line and then raced across the empty runway, legs pumping as hard as if I were in a hundred yard dash.

'Hey, you!' a policeman shouted. 'Get back!' From the corner of my eye I saw his blue uniform heading towards me. The asphalt seemed to stick to my shoes and the soft tarmac was like a swamp.

'Dad!' I shouted. 'It's me!' My father looked in my direction but I don't think he recognized me. I was still too far away. 'Dad!' Just then I was grabbed by the shoulder, spun around and pushed to the ground. My elbows banged against the asphalt, which wasn't as soft as it looked. The crowd roared and then it seemed as if the whole airport was shifting and moving. Legs rose and fell, people yelled, hands waved in the air. A small stampede of men hurtled protectively towards me, their feet chattering strangely on the tarmac. I saw a shoe fly into the air. The lone policeman abandoned me, put up his arms and crouched defensively, but that was not enough to stop the onslaught. Hands grabbed him and with the weight of their bodies the men brought him down. I didn't see what happened next because Yorgo had suddenly picked me up and, with Jason running alongside, he bounded like a panther

79

towards the airport building, all the while kissing me and shouting, 'You silly brave kid! You silly kid!'

Yorgo ordered us into a black Dodge that stopped right in front of us. When I looked back through the rear window I saw, strewn across the tarmac, a scattering of shoes and bits of cloth. More policemen were arriving and the crowd was dispersing, running in twenty directions. Jason caught a hurried glimpse of my father bending down to get into a Mercedes. 'Dad's OK!' He pointed to a man being dragged into a van. 'Wow!' he said. 'Look at what you started.'

In the back seat we replayed scenes for each other, jabbering out endless didja see thises and didja see thats and Holy Majolies and Great Cannellonies. Jason went whump! imitating a club hitting a man, I went pow! and bent over as if I'd been punched in the stomach, and soon we were scrambling all over the place, performing strangleholds and half-nelsons and karate chops.

'Skasmos! Isihia!' Yorgo told us to shut up and calm down. Meekly I stared out of the window while Jason slumped over the front seat and talked. Just before we reached home Yorgo patted my head, pinched my cheeks, shook his head and said, 'Po! Po! Would you believe it? The son shamed us all.'

When we arrived at our house in Psyhiko my father was already there and when he saw us he freed himself from a small group of men and hugged us. Then he asked to see me alone. I followed his heavy steps up the wooden stairs that led to his attic office.

'Not a very smart thing you did today,' he began. From a

leather pouch he extracted some fingerfuls of fresh tobacco, which looked like strands of curly hair, and packed it into the pipe. He flicked the lighter off and let loose a stream of smoke. I inhaled with him. 'You started something like a riot.'

I hung my head with a certain mischievous pride, like the war hero who breaks the rules to save his squadron. If Jason and Yorgo were so proud of me, my father couldn't be far behind.

'You could have gotten yourself hurt.'

I nodded my head. I expected my fair punishment.

'Do you agree you did something foolish?'

Again I nodded.

'Crowds are dangerous. Do you know why they raced towards the aeroplane?' He leaned towards me and the leather squeaked. 'Because they saw what I saw, a man running towards me, a man unafraid of authority.'

From his window I could make out, through the haze of heat, the Acropolis, sitting imperiously above the city. 'I was helping the Athenians against the Spartans, Dad.' He raised an eyebrow. 'Not the people of Athens. The Athenians, you know, like in ancient history.'

He laughed. 'Father would like to hear that.' He tousled my hair. 'Athenians versus the Spartans,' he mused, more to himself than to me.

'There's something else I'd like to say,' he continued. He walked over to the window and stared out. 'Something I usually don't have time to think about.'

Suddenly Yorgo popped his head in. Reporters wanted

answers, he said. My father waved him off, but Yorgo insisted it was urgent. They wanted to know whether the police had come to the airport to arrest him. Had they provoked a riot so that they could accuse him of inciting violence? My father turned to me and said he would continue the discussion another time.

Over the years that event at the airport grew in importance. My father would tell his friends about it at dinner, each time slightly differently. Sometimes the police were in the hundreds or the crowds were in the thousands, sometimes the small battle was a massive riot. Sometimes I broke free from the policeman and made it to the stairway. I realize now that it was far easier for him to let the great many know how he felt about me than to tell me directly, when it was just the two of us together in a room.

Once he even told the part about the Spartans and the Athenians to a large crowd in an auditorium. They laughed and applauded. Perhaps that was the closest he ever came to picking up the discussion that Yorgo had interrupted that hot day in September.

8 *Athens by Night*

The *fanatikos* we worried about finally showed up at our house one dark night, but not alone. He was an officer in the Greek military and brought with him about twenty soldiers, two military trucks and a tank whose heavy engine throbbed in our chests. From the third-floor attic room where I slept with Jason, I heard pounding on the door, someone shouting our father's name, and my mother's accented Greek, telling them my father wasn't in the house.

Jason and I knew where our father was. Just minutes earlier he had run into our room wearing only his trunks. From the balcony of our room Jason helped him on to the roof, lifting him up with a great heave-ho, while I kept watch at the top of the stairs. When the soldiers stomped into our room – after crashing up the wooden stairs so loudly I thought the whole stairway would collapse from their weight – I smelled something like onions. This was the smell of men in heat. The officer in the black beret came last, dressed in olive-green pants which ballooned over his boots, shouting my father's name hysterically, over and over. Saliva flew from his mouth and his Adam's apple – ribbed like a grenade – danced up and down. The shelves of books, the heavy oak desk, the set of pipes hanging from the pipe-holder, the sheets of paper, me and Jason, each object seemed to send charges of electricity into his nervous system. His jerky movements made it look as if there was a wire inside his body which was difficult to bend. From the wall he tore down my grandfather's picture, stomped on it and sent shards of glass into the air. He kicked in the closet doors, swiped the pipes off the desk and sniffed my father's tobacco. With the help of two soldiers, he cleared all the books from the shelves, tumbling them into a heap on the floor. One book he held on to and, with a tremendous effort, roaring my father's name, tore in half. Leaning forward, hands behind his back he paced in front of me and Jason.

'Where is he?' He bent even lower and sniffed Jason's head.

'We don't know,' Jason replied. After this storm, Jason's voice was like a quiet day. The officer stood back, drew the revolver from his belt and brought the muzzle to Jason's temple.

'Now will you tell me where he is?' The officer was breathing hard as if he'd been running. Jason's mouth was shut tight and his lips formed a thin line as he shook his head. Suddenly everything slowed down, and I felt as if I was watching a movie. I noticed the raised brand name on the gun barrel; the pulse of the vein in Jason's temple looked like a mole burrowing under the ground. In the distance a soldier leaned his rifle against his body, lifted up his glasses, wiped his nose and replaced the glasses; at any other time this would have been a normal gesture but now its very normality, with the gun pressed against Jason's head, made it seem macabre, made the gun all too real, all too possible.

'It's me you want,' said a familiar voice, 'not him.' My father had abandoned his hiding place.

The officer returned the revolver to his holster and then, as if released from some strange internal prison, he started hopping up and down, shouting, 'We have you! We have you!' Suddenly he stopped, straightened his shirt and saluted my father. 'You're under arrest!' he said in a loud voice, standing so straight you would have thought this was the high point of his career.

The first sign that Jason blamed himself for our father's arrest was his belief that he was contracting fatal diseases. In the middle of dinner he'd stop chewing his food, touch his face and tell my mother that his jaw felt too heavy to go on eating – because he'd contracted lockjaw from some mongrel. He massaged his head, convinced that somewhere inside it a tumour was growing. Sometimes he sat in a chair, head forward, pretending to be catatonic, and claimed that his body was 'shutting down'. He read about a disease you could get from old bones and recalled that last year in Patras, on some trip with our father, we'd kissed the skull of St Andreas. Certain that this disease led to some sort of hidden ageing of his veins, he stared at his eyes for signs they were growing prematurely old, and once shone a light in my eyes to compare them with his, convinced he was seeing the world through the darkening vision of an eighty-year-old man.

But very soon the fear of diseases faded away and he started to court death in a different way. He would challenge his friends to run in front of speeding cars, and the winner was the one who came closest to the car's bumper. He always won. He would race down a steep hill on his bicycle and jump off into a haystack while the bicycle continued on its own like a headless rider.

One Wednesday afternoon in the auditorium of Athens College – Jason was in the tenth grade and I was in the sixth – we listened to a lieutenant lecture on civics. His lesson went beyond the new constitution and the 'restricted but also expanded' rights of the citizen. 'Did you know that they used gypsy nails to crucify Christ?' he asked us, and pointed to the ancient map of Israel and Palestine. 'Did you know that the man who brought Jesus the vinegar sponge was black? Did you know it was Jews who stoned him?' The officer said that Judas, Herod, Plato, and the hippies in America were all linked to Communism and Socialism and to Greeks like our father. I think he knew that we were in the audience. 'I'll show them,' Jason said as we walked home that day.

Not long after that, Jason started to disappear from our room at night. He would wait for our mother to go to sleep and then creep out of the house, appearing early the next morning. He would go back to bed for a couple of hours but was barely able to keep his head up at breakfast. I asked him to tell me what he was up to but he merely smiled and looked away.

One night he woke me up.

'Athens by night?' There was a strange look on his face but at the time I was so proud that he wanted to include me that I didn't think about it. I don't know why he wanted me to come along. Perhaps to show me just how much he had changed. No matter, I dressed quickly, followed him out of the kitchen door and we raced through the gardens of other houses before reaching the streets. The evening was quiet; the moon was bright. The headlights of a car sent us running behind a tree. It was like being in a spy movie.

When we came to a park with chestnut trees, Jason plunged into the darkness and I followed. He searched out a low, leafy bush and then crawled in on his knees and emerged with a pail, two bottles of water, a brush and a pouch. The brush had thick bristles and a bony wooden handle, resembling a short-handled broom. 'This is the best the "organization" can afford,' Jason told me knowingly, allowing me to draw even closer to him.

He mixed the contents of the pouch with the water and we made our way back to the street and arrived in front of the massive walls of Arsakio, the private girls' school.

'This is our canvas,' Jason said.

I held the pail while he dipped the brush. The wall was old and stubbly and absorbed the gypsum paint without leaving much of a trace. Jason had to paint each letter three times. In the curfew-quiet of the evening, the brush swished along the wall like a cat's hard tongue licking skin.

A truck roared in the distance. We crouched low against the wall, but there was really no place to hide. We squeezed close to each other and tucked our heads to our knees until the sound faded. I pressed my face so hard against the wall that I chafed my cheek.

By the third word we were low on whitewash so we up-ended the pail and let the lumpy concoction drip slowly on to the brush. We were so busy concentrating on the mechanics of painting that we didn't hear tyres swish along the asphalt. Two doors slammed in the night and then we heard the hard crunch of feet on the street. The wall extended in both direc-tions. A voice told us to stand up slowly and keep our hands down while a light was shone on our faces. I brought my hands to my sides and stood at attention, like in school. I could see their black shoes at the edge of the darkness. The paint dripped down the wall and my lungs burned from its musty smell. One of them thwacked his club against his thigh. Each time the club came down against his thigh, coins jangled in his pocket.

Suddenly, as if he'd made up his mind, he asked us our names. I looked at Jason who shook his head at me, but then told them our names, partly to prevent Jason from having to act the hero. Hearing the fear in my voice, I grew even more afraid.

'It's me you want,' Jason said. 'Not him. He's not even eleven.' I felt his body next to mine, though not his warmth. The men spoke in low tones and then ordered us into the back seat of the police car. I didn't even think of running away. The seats were torn; Styrofoam stuck out through the cracks. They smelled of sweat and vomit. I tried to open the window but there was no handle. The driver was balding and his nose looked like it had been pushed into his face. The other man had thick eyebrows and a neck that joined to his chin, like a worm.

They drove so slowly I was sure they were doing it on purpose. I strained to distinguish familiar houses. I reached out and held my brother's hand. He gave me a strong squeeze and then let go. This was the last time I was seeing these streets, I decided. I would never see my mother again. Oh, please don't torture us, I thought, we're still little, I don't want to grow old very fast, I don't want to walk on crutches. Why had I been so stupid tonight? Why had I come along? He didn't care if we were caught. Why don't they let me out of the car and I swear I'll fight for Jason. I knew why the back seat smelled of vomit, because people got afraid and when they were afraid they did things like that.

We passed the black fencing of a friend's house. We were driving in a circle! I sensed my father reaching out from his lonely gaol cell with long invisible arms, protecting us with a shield. As long as he was alive, I would be all right. Suddenly the driver stopped the car, got out, opened the door and said, 'You can go.' I jumped out and landed hard on my hands and knees but didn't feel a thing. 'This one stays.' I pressed my face to the cold hard window.

Jason was sitting in the back seat with his arms folded across his chest like the police were his private chauffeurs. The car took off; its red tail-lights grew smaller and then were lost in the streets of Psyhiko.

I stood in the middle of the road and stared at the moon rising behind the ragged peaks of the chestnut trees. I ran through the streets. I stumbled more than once, scraped my knees, grazed my palms, but picked myself up and continued running.

When I got home I was surprised to see the police car outside our house, its lights on. The two officers were holding Jason in their arms. His body was limp, his head hung forward and his feet dangled loosely. One of them rapped on our door with his club. I crouched behind a bush which gave off a rich dewy smell. When my mother opened the door she let out a cry, a strange high-pitched cry that rang out in the stillness of the night like a curse.

When the car pulled away I raced inside through the kitchen door – which we always kept open. My mother was laying Jason down on the couch. There were tears in her eyes and she was muttering something. I swarmed around her, jumping up and down. 'Is he all right? Is he all right? Mom, is he alive?' My mother dabbed his face with a wet hand-kerchief. An enormous red welt rose on his cheek and his upper lip was bloated and shiny.

My mother let out a sob as she dabbed his lip with an awful-smelling yellow ointment. I sat on the edge of the couch and cried like the child I decided I was.

For his own protection, because he continued to prowl the streets at night and conspire with friends his age, my mother sent Jason out of the country, to live with his American grandparents in Chicago. We lost touch with each other and grew up separately. When our family went into exile in Canada he was already attending an American college in Massachusetts.

This was the end of the 1960s. Jason grew his hair long, wore clogs that added three inches to his height, wore ban-

dannas, grew a beard, and pinned protest buttons to his shirt
and pants. He played the guitar, learned ju-jitsu, and worked
in the college cafeteria. He hitch-hiked all over the eastern
seaboard to join protests against the Vietnam war, and
switched from maths to the humanities.

We returned to Greece once the dictators were behind
bars. Our old neighbourhood had changed: the walls on
which Jason and I had painted 'Democracy will w . . .' had
been torn down, to make way for the Bulgarian embassy, but
the park with chestnuts was still there. A great number of
people started to arrive at our home – to greet and touch my
father – bringing with them bits and pieces of the old Greece.
The house was filled with their voices, their smells, their gifts
and requests, their hopes. They slept in our bedrooms, in the
kitchen, in the living room and gathered sometimes even in
the bathrooms to discuss the forthcoming election campaign,
the first in nine years. Upon his return Jason cut his hair short,
gave up his guitar-playing, lost the clogs and ran for deputy in
the Greek parliament.

With a backpack from his hitch-hiking years he visited the
villages of Peloponnesus. A politician sleeping outdoors in a
sleeping bag, living from the contents of a backpack, unafraid
of physical threats made by the village fanatics – this was
something new for most people. He came first in his district.

After the elections I went to the Greek parliament to watch
him being sworn in. Jason, one of the youngest deputies ever
to enter these halls, shifted uncomfortably throughout the
swearing-in ceremony. Sitting among all those other dark-
suited men with their thick moustaches yellowing at the ends

from nicotine, their braces, fobs and easy manners, Jason looked foreign. Their trousers, pocketless at the back, hugged their hips, and their jackets seemed too tight. Jason's suit was loose; his trousers rode high, and his jacket was comfortably large. Maybe he was just one more face among many, but his was a face unblemished by smoke, bright as a light. He sat four rows behind our father, the party leader, in this way making his first quiet statement.

I think I was a little jealous of him but also relieved that it was him standing there and not me, that it was him locked for ever into my father's world, not me. 'It's me you want,' he had said years ago, 'not him.' I don't think he ever expected to end up here.

What had he been thinking when he walked into parliament with our father, I asked him when the session was over, while we stood in one of the panelled halls of the parliament building. His face took on that calm, impenetrable expression.

'Here is the future,' he said.

'That's a politician talking,' I said, 'not a brother.'

He lifted his eyebrows, rubbed his chin and smiled the way he'd learn to smile in front of crowds, and then, as if he was worried of showing signs of premature ageing in his eyes – like he had years ago when he thought he saw the world through the darkening vision of an eighty-year-old – he looked away.

9 *By the Light of the Pall Malls*

During the years before the dictatorship, when both my father and grandfather were running the government or campaigning to get back into it, when slogans like 'The king reigns and the people govern!' were common, our kitchen resembled Larissis Square, the bustling Athens train depot. At any time of the day I was certain to encounter workers with cement-encrusted shoes, villagers smelling of olive oil and retsina, well-dressed gentlemen in black hats, high-school teachers with handlebar moustaches, tough-looking guys with amber worry beads who sat down in the kitchen as if they owned it and covered the kitchen table with their arms, and women who sat tidily in one place and held their heads low and called me 'sir'. One of them was sure to have brought herbs and explained their uses – nettle (for blood and kidney), absinth (digestion), balsam (sleeplessness), eucalyptus (breathing), oregano (muscle cramps) and hyssop (rheumatism).

After my father's arrest the good people of Greece no longer showed up on our doorstep. Few dared come to a political prisoner's home. The only kids my mother got to come for my eleventh birthday were those whose fathers were already in jail. So, one evening, when we heard a knock on the front door, it was such a surprise that Lydia, my mother and I went together to answer it, wondering who it might be.

A man stood in the doorway, resting on crutches. Behind him I heard the clunky sound of a diesel taxi, waiting. The man's hair was sparse and wispy and his cheeks sunken. The skin of his bare arms seemed to be losing some of its colour, as if someone had scraped off a top layer to expose another one beneath it and the two colours met in a ragged border of skin.

My mother hugged him. 'Yorgo!' she said. His large eyes were familiar but I still didn't know who it was. He leaned heavily against my mother and his hands clenched and un-clenched the horizontal grip of the crutches like a pump. His face broke into a grimace. Suddenly I recognized him. It was the Yorgo who came from my grandfather's village, the one who thought Lydia was such a beautiful granddaughter. Before the arrest, at the time he worked as my father's sec-retary, he had been a man of vigour who danced at the slight-est excuse, always smiled, spoke in a friendly voice and seemed to have an interest in us children that went beyond mere patronizing of my father. In those days he had had a headful of black hair, a full moustache and playful eyes.

We sat at the wooden table in the kitchen – ever since the arrest we no longer entered the living room. My mother brought Yorgo sweet *koulouria* and a small cup of Greek coffee. He sipped the coffee, bending very low, inhaled its smell, and sighed. Then, when he finished with the coffee, he held out his hands and examined them from both sides as if they were for sale, tucked them into his shirt, brought them out again, put them on the table and stared at them. They were skinny, bony hands, with a network of lumpy veins.

'I thought of you and the children many times,' he said finally, looking at Lydia and me. I wondered how long it had been since he'd had a coffee; I wondered if they'd put drugs in his food to make him talk, though I had no idea what he might talk about. Suddenly he reached out and touched my cheek. This was unexpected. I pulled back so the tips of his fingers – his fingernails really – just brushed against my skin. I imagined red lines where he touched me.

'Sorry, I'm very sorry. I must go,' he said and started to rise from his chair. My face grew hot. It was my fault he was leaving. My mother didn't insist he stay. Immediately she retrieved the crutches from behind the kitchen door and waited for him to stand to place them under his arms. Her quick, efficient movements and her sideways glances at us made me think she didn't want him to stay any longer, either. We shuffled with him to the door and as soon as we opened it the taxi's engine sputtered to life. When he leaned over on his crutches to kiss me, I made sure I didn't pull back. After she closed the door I rubbed my burning face.

'Let's have an apple,' my mother said with very little enthusiasm. With her nail she removed a soft brown spot, then peeled the apple, sliced it open, dug out the black pips and gave us each a piece.

'Are they torturing Dad?' I asked.

She didn't look at me. Instead she retrieved a pack of

filterless Pall Malls from the top of the refrigerator and tapped the box on the edge of the table to loosen a cigarette. Then she stopped, rose from the table, threw the pack into her handbag and, with brisk movements, drew out the car keys and jangled the car keys in front of us.

'Cigarette trip?'

My heart leapt. Being out on the streets at this time of night was dangerous, but tonight was different. We had seen Yorgo. And, besides, we did have some form of protection: Californian licence plates. If the licence plates weren't enough and we were stopped, she told us to pretend we didn't understand Greek. We had to hope we weren't recognized.

We left all the lights on to make it look as if someone was still in the house, and my mother drove the car out of the garage. Lydia and I looked both ways down the street and told her when to pull out without being seen. We hopped in and drove fast through the cypress-lined streets of Psyhiko, slowing down only once we reached the main boulevard of Kiffisias Street. Most of the traffic consisted of military trucks and squat jeeps. Soldiers stood at major intersections. Our mother told us that the military were afraid of places where people gathered, even red traffic lights. I liked the way she could turn things around. I had thought soldiers in their green uniforms, with their blue helmets and bayoneted rifles, could only be a sign of strength.

We stopped next to a shuttered kiosk and stood in the shadows of its orange awning. Directly across the street was the Averoff Prison, a reddish building built before the First World War which resembled a medieval castle, with rolls of barbed wire along the top of the walls, and guards standing inside the turrets at each of the four corners.

Father in jail. I recalled how only a few months earlier when he was still free he had come into the bedroom to kiss me goodnight. He sat on the edge of my bed. This was a rare visit and I felt privileged. He sat in silence, hands folded calmly in his lap.

'I might be in jail soon,' he said finally. His voice was even, the kind of voice that calmed people down, not the voice he used when he was angry or speaking to a crowd from the balcony.

'Have you done something wrong?'

He laughed. I asked him who would come to get him, with all the crowds who gathered for his speeches and all the people visiting us each day in the kitchen.

'Everybody's a friend, Alex. But when the skies turn dark, people pretend they can't see you.'

Cars drove slowly down the wide boulevard. From her white leather bag my mother drew out a pack of Pall Malls. We didn't know for sure, but an amnestied prisoner had told my mother that my father's cell faced the road. Since then, every other day, just before the curfew began, she would stand next to the kiosk and light her cigarette. She told us that her reward was the tiny glow of another cigarette from behind the bars of one of the cells.

In the gloom the vertical bars of the cell windows dropped like black daggers. I watched my mother smoke the Pall Mall down to nothing in long, extended puffs. The glow curled back along the cigarette. She coughed and lit up another.

'Maybe he's sleeping,' Lydia said.

I didn't want to think of my father on crutches, hands scrabbling urgently at the Pall Mall package. My mother squeezed the cigarette hard with her fingers and puffed smoke. I peered across the street into the darkness. In the distance came a low rumble of trucks. My mother threw her cigarette down and pulled out another. She was about to light it when Lydia said, '*Phos!* A light! A light! Look. Do you see it?'

Just then the convoy of trucks drove by and blocked our view. It seemed to take for ever to pass. I tried to peer through the spaces between each passing truck but their bright headlights made everything but the street invisible. When the convoy finally passed the three of us craned our necks forward like birds. All I could see was the looming darkness of the prison. No light, no glow.

'What do they do when they torture you?' I asked Jason one day. I hoped that he didn't know the answer. I also hoped he did. I wanted to possess the knowledge of torture without having to learn it, I wanted it to be there, but tucked away in a safe corner to be retrieved only when absolutely necessary. The things he told me sounded too strange to imagine. The worst one of all, I decided, was the stuff they did to your teeth without anaesthesia. I could hear the whining sound of the drill shifting down an octave as it bit into bone.

'Do you think they're torturing Dad?'

'Nope,' Jason said, like an adult who knew everything. 'He

has important friends in America who stopped the torture after the first night.' I didn't pursue it. His answer was good enough for me, I didn't want to be disappointed by pushing him on details and discovering that he was lying.

While Jason slept in the bed I tried to imagine what it was like to be beaten. Palm against the front of my nose, I applied pressure, pushing back and up. What did it mean to break your nose? Could you breathe with a broken nose, would the broken part block the air coming from the nostrils, would you be swallowing blood? I bit my lip. Not hard enough to make it hurt. Something prevented me. I punched myself lightly in the stomach. This didn't hurt at all. I tried a stronger punch, then an even stronger one. I closed my eyes, relaxed and then as if to surprise myself, brought my fist into my thorax as hard as I could. That knocked the wind out of me and I keeled over. It hurt.

There wasn't some inviolable rule that prevented you from doing damage, like the robots in science fiction stories that were programmed not to damage themselves. If you could cause pain to yourself, you could cause pain to someone else. That was probably how torture worked.

The next day I decided to act. I retrieved two packs of Pall Malls from the cartons my mother had bought at the American Club in Kifissia. In my grip they gave me a peculiar sense of power. I thrust them into my pocket, left the house and rode my bike in search of the Wild Man of Psyhiko.

I'd seen him on the streets a few times and was a little afraid of him. I had heard from the kiosk man that he would stand on the sidewalks and shout at passing cars, 'Long live democracy! Down with the dictators!' He had hair that stuck up in the air, porcupine eyebrows, wore a ragged suit with loose shirt-tails, and his toes protruded from his shoes. After shouting a slogan, he would bring his hand to his mouth, crouch, and look around in fear. The words escaped from him of their own volition, it seemed. Our mother said he was suffering from a peculiar form of Tourette's syndrome, a disease that compels those afflicted with it to swear and say dirty words all the time, except that under a dictatorship words like 'freedom' and 'democracy' were dirty and the ones he couldn't help from shouting. He reminded me a little of Manoli, who used to speak to himself. The police would beat him up, get him to promise not to shout any more, and release him a few days later. He would disappear for weeks and then appear once more, standing at the side of the road, at first only muttering and grumbling, then kicking tin cans, until finally he couldn't hold back any longer and would explode into cries and slogans.

In Eucalyptus Square I stopped and asked the kiosk owner, who knew me, if he'd seen the Wild Man. The kiosk owner, one of those who used to visit our kitchen, was solidly built and wore a colourful short-sleeved shirt. I think he was curious but he didn't ask why I wanted to know. He'd passed by in the morning, he told me, and was probably somewhere nearby. He leaned towards me and whispered, 'Don't worry. One day your father will get his revenge.'

Chewing a stick of gum he had given me, and armed with my Pall Malls, I rode up Tsakona Street. I found him in the Palia Agora, mouthing words but making no sound. He was waving a hand in the air as if giving a speech. His complexion was splotchy and his left arm dangled at his side.

He didn't notice me at first. When he saw me he hooted in surprise, then glanced over his shoulder. I held out the packets. He, of all people, would recognize their magical properties. He stared at them for a moment and then, with a quick movement, snatched them from my hands and lifted them triumphantly into the air.

'Down with torture!' he shouted. 'Long live Pall Mall!'

10   *As Much As You Can*

Sometimes when Jason and I returned from Athens College
we would find my mother writing letters to congressmen and
senators like Fulbright and Robert Kennedy, to academics
like Carl Kaysen and John Kenneth Galbraith and to President
Johnson, asking them to help free her husband from jail. The
first time she read us one of those letters, we kids listened as if
each word were bringing my father closer to freedom, so
convinced were we of the power of our other country. When
she sealed each envelope and placed the stamp on the upper
right corner, we were thrilled. Sometimes she would let me
give the letter to the postman and impatiently I would watch
him ride his bicycle down the street, already imagining the
letter firmly in the hands of some famous American who
would immediately set my father free.

Other times we would return from school and she would
be alone in the kitchen, staring out of the window. She had
taken to wearing a black scarf over her head and never went
without her thick black sunglasses that made her look like
Onassis, we joked. If someone phoned, she would ask, 'Any
news?' and after a pause she would usually say something like,

'No, just checking, that's all right.' People would phone and say they'd heard my father was being released. The first time we heard that we were so happy; we learned to restrain ourselves the following times. She smoked more and drew on the Pall Malls with long hard puffs, the same way she smoked when she stood outside the prison at night in case my father could see the glow of her cigarette from his cell. One day she spent hours carefully putting all the pictures of one of my father's election campaigns into an album and the next day she tore them out and threw them back into the cardboard box. For us children our father's absence was not so strange since he had always been away from the house, on the campaign trail, meeting people in his office, staying in Parliament until late at night, and even when he was at home, it was usually with dozens of others. But I knew that for my mother each day that he remained in jail was a blow to her heart.

One morning three men from 'internal security' arrived at our house. Two of them were young, athletic-looking, with their hair cropped short and wearing tight-fitting suits, shiny black shoes and white socks. The third, with grey wispy hair, apologized for their presence. His belt was cinched tight and the excess hung like a tongue from his waist. He didn't wear sunglasses like the others, which meant he didn't care that one day we might recognize him.

He sat with my mother in the kitchen and gently asked me to leave. I did, but put my ear to the wooden door. Jason and Lydia were not in the house, otherwise I would have called them to join me. I imagined my mother sitting across from the man while the other security men stared out of the window and pretended to be checking on something, whereas they were actually listening to my mother very carefully, recording her movements, the intonation of her voice, searching for signs that she was lying. I pressed my ear so hard against the door it stung.

'Why do you want to hurt Greece?' I heard him ask. He knew that she stood outside the prison at night, lighting up cigarettes. Was she using Morse code? What did she know of the king's coup attempt? If she wasn't forthcoming, they would move his cell. So it really was my father up there with the glowing cigarette. That was the first time we had any confirmation that he could see us.

Her letters made Greece look bad. 'Don't you love Greece?' Then he paused and maybe he walked around because I heard footsteps pacing the floor. When he sat down again he spoke in a low monotone, but his voice sounded triumphant. I heard scattered words: 'wavy chestnut hair', 'medium height', names of restaurants and hotels, and then numbers: 'five-ten sixty-four,' or 'one twelve sixty-five'. These were dates the way security men said them. He said something about 'full breasts' and suddenly I remembered seeing an unknown woman breast-feeding a baby in his bedroom. She had looked at me but hadn't bothered to cover herself up. The sudden sight of her swollen breast had taken my breath away.

'He's Greek. You're an American. One day he'll leave you.' There was silence. Then I heard the hard squeak of a chair. Movement, then my mother's voice, so low and harsh that I thought it was someone else talking. I pictured her standing now, her face red, shaking her hand at him and showing him the door. I pulled away just in time. I had hoped to see the man angry but he came out slowly, looked at me with vague eyes, took a long pull on his cigarette and dropped it on the floor. I waited for them to leave before putting it out, grinding it hard with my heel.

When I heard their car pull away, I ran into the kitchen. My mother was sitting on the wooden chair, staring out of the window. She didn't seem to hear me come in. She stared at her hands like an old woman. I stood next to her and heard her deep inhalations. I coughed and she looked up at me as if only now realizing I was in the kitchen. She pulled me close, but it seemed only a reflex.

She held me for a while. Then she began to talk, more to herself than to me, I thought. Some governments, she said, separate husbands from their wives for years, tell them lies, write false letters, get women to call wives. 'The family is a natural cell of resistance,' she said, 'and they want to break that resistance down. That's why they were here.'

'But it didn't work, did it?' I said hesitantly, recalling the unknown woman in my father's bedroom.

She wasn't listening.

I ventured a little further. 'I was listening through the door.'

'Then you know it's all lies,' she said and then got up quickly as if she had something important to do.

My mother's letters to American senators and to my father's important friends in America, the extent of his influence in Greece, and the international media publicity served as a protective mantle while he remained in prison. My mother used her American citizenship as if it was made of gold – and it was. That our private lives were so very public was a good thing. But not all good. In a Cavafy poem I had read that you should try – as much as you can – not to degrade your life through too much contact with the world because it grows tattered, like clothes worn too often. But what choice did we have but to let everybody see us, touch, sniff and rub? That was our protection.

Over the radio one Saturday we heard the announcement that all political prisoners were going to be amnestied, including my father. The day of his release people started to show up at our home, almost like they used to. The first to arrive were Vassilis, who owned the kiosk, our gardener, the maid, and Yorgo, who needed only one crutch now. His hair was darker and fuller than when he'd just come out of prison. There was Stratis, a distant cousin whom we hadn't seen in years, wearing a dapper-looking silk scarf around his neck, and my godfather in his three-piece suit, puffing on his pipe.

When I entered the kitchen there were a number of strangers sitting around the table sipping coffee and smoking heavily. A fat man with hair growing along his nape like a horse's mane took pictures of us with a Leica. A grey-haired man whistled resistance songs through his two gold teeth and took it upon himself to adjust the paintings on our walls. Two villagers from my grandfather's birthplace had brought us four stuffed hares, a jug of olives, and yoghurt pie. And more kept arriving. Even Yorgo's taxi-driver, who parked the car half-on half-off the pavement, was boiling Greek coffee in a *briki*.

Earlier that day my mother had flung open the living-room windows – closed for the duration – to let in the bright Athenian sun. Now these people darkened the rooms, cluttered the hallways and filled the house with their smoke, their voices and their smells. Suddenly all of Greece showing up on our doorstep didn't seem such a great thing.

I raced out of the house and hopped on to my bicycle. Riding hard, I pedalled vigorously down Gizi Street, turned up Papparigopoulou and reached the park with the birch trees. The park was still and deserted; the ground was strewn with twisted strips of bark and smelled of earth. The sun was up but it was a false December sun and I was cold. I walked with no purpose among the trees, hands deep in my pockets, every now and then kicking a pine-cone.

This was the first time I had ever sought out a moment for myself, even if I wasn't aware, at the age of eleven, that such moments were called 'private'. The Greek language has no word for 'privacy', except for the word *idiotes*, which means private citizen, the one who is not interested in society and not involved in politics, from which we get the word 'idiot'. I imagined what things would be like now my father was coming back. In his absence I had visited his office many times to smell his tobacco. I had stood in front of his wardrobe and run my fingers along his silk ties and once I even polished his shoes. Now, walking aimlessly through the park, I could already hear the buzz of people that followed him and I could see the small groups appearing at our doorstep at all hours of the day.

Suddenly I panicked. I was certain that my father would

arrive in my absence. I hopped on to my bike and rode back fast, standing up on the pedals.

I couldn't have imagined that twenty-five years later, having escaped the fish bowl of publicity for the soothing anonymity of a large American city, I would turn on the television and watch my mother being interviewed by a popular talk-show hostess. The topic was older men divorcing their wives for younger women. By then the dictators were in the Korydallos jail, my father had risen more than once to the pinnacle of power in Greece, and had fallen precisely because of his marriage to a much younger woman and had then risen again – and our lives had become common property.

In a measured voice my mother said she would have preferred her divorce – and she was certain any woman would prefer this – to be a private affair. When the hostess asked if she wanted revenge on my father for marrying a younger woman after more than forty years of marriage – and here I could imagine the audience leaning forward – my mother replied, 'I guess it's very simple. Now that it's over, there's only one thing that counts.' She paused and the studio audience grew silent. 'I still love him.'

I heard groans from the audience. I thought of the Cavafy poem. What was my mother doing? The television panned over the audience, mainly women, some of whom had raised their hands eagerly to get a chance at the microphone. The hostess pointed to one of them, a young woman in a blue blazer. She rose to the mike.

'Love, I tried that.' She paused for the laughter to subside.

'It doesn't really work,' she continued in a chirpy, self-confident voice, 'especially these days.'

I wanted to jump into that crowd. I wanted to tell this woman otherwise, I wanted to speak from the weight of memory. I, at least, had seen love at work, I had seen love bring my father home. But this woman was right about one thing. It *was* a long time ago: 24 December 1967, to be exact.

On that cool, cloudless evening, I waited impatiently in the doorway of our house. Yorgo's crutch pressed against my back as we gathered in the doorway, my brother Jason swayed against me, and Lydia and Hector jostled for position. I stood in front of them to make sure I would be the first to greet my father.

Finally we heard sirens. A convoy of police cars screeched to a halt. My father got out and stood for a little before shutting the door slowly. He walked up the steps. None of us moved. Instead we huddled under the doorway in cloistered silence. Until he had crossed some invisible threshold we couldn't believe he was here. Then the cars drove off. That was the signal. I leapt out at him. With a shout of joy he lifted Hector and me up in the air and did a little circle with us. No teeth were missing. He was all right. He put us down, hugged Jason and lifted my sister into the air as well and whispered something into her ear. Then he put Lydia down and turned to my mother. I believed it was she who had brought him home safe, with the strength of her love, making our family – as much as she could – the natural cell of resistance. He must have believed it too, the way he hugged her hard, the way he kissed her, before he was swallowed up by all the people who wanted him so very much.

11   *Lambda is for Laothalassa*

When we first moved to Greece, my father's mother, who lived with us, took on the task of improving our Greek. To grow into who we were, my grandmother said, meant learning Greek. She gave us Greek books to read but above all she insisted we learn to write Greek 'beautifully'. She was determined, on this at least, not to let her grandchildren get away with the sloppy American writing habits acquired in the California public-school system. 'An elegant writing style,' she said in her precise, formal Greek, 'is a necessity in today's world.'

So began the calligraphy lessons. Once a week I sat at her small ebony-coloured desk – she always made sure my shoulders were straight and that when I leaned forward I did so without bending my back – and then she would place in front of me some fresh, creamy-smelling sheets of paper, an inkwell, and a stylus with removable nibs. For these occasions she wore not her ornate ruffled blouse and stylish *chapeau* but some loose equivalent of an older woman's workclothes: a long grey woollen skirt that reached her ankles, with two sets of enormous buttons running its length, and a simple white blouse.

We began with the Greek alphabet. She showed me how to ornament each letter with its own particular curlicue and wisp, adding tails, lengthening stalks, thickening stems and thinning curves by twisting and turning the nib of the stylus. I learned to taper downstrokes and add flourishes to upward strokes – descenders and ascenders she called them; she made me concentrate on initial and terminal letters so that I could lend them 'grace and freedom', and she showed me how to connect two letters with a smooth ligature. She corrected me if I didn't hold the pen properly, because it wasn't enough that the letters look beautiful but that I look good while engaged in the act of writing. If someone should come in while I was writing, they should notice the elegant way I held the pen, angled back like a reed bending in the wind, not sticking crassly up in the air like the mast of a ship. She showed me how to dip the nib into ink and turn it slightly so it wouldn't drip on the creamy white sheet, to check for the watermark on the paper and to imagine a horizontal line running through each word. While she taught me the art of calligraphy she also taught me about each letter's 'soul', as she put it, its *psyche*.

I learned that each letter has its own personality. The letter lambda (λ) has two legs which dangle beneath the word. A properly drawn lambda is a wonderful thing, a lovely trigonometer; think of lambda like a little man leaning forward so that you draw the first leg slightly shorter than the second. Lambda's embarrassed to be such a beautiful letter, which is why we draw its head slightly bowed and why it keeps its hands in its pockets. If you lift lambda by its head and shake it like a bell, the sound drops out of it – *ul ul ul*. I could see myself as a lambda, hands in pockets, head down.

The letter beta (β) was pregnant twelve months of the year; pie (π) was a square block of a letter shaped like a house; only something as solid as that could shelter the equation for the area of the circle, a shape which so intrigued the ancient Greeks. Psi (ψ) was like Poseidon's trident, clearly a masculine letter, one that could be used to spear fish. Open your mouth for capital omega (Ω), feel it, the large drawn-out *ooh* sound versus its taut, breathless brother omicron that looked like your mouth when you pronounced it. There was the delicate delta (δ) and the cantankerous eta (η). The small gamma (γ) was a scissors while its capitalized version resembled a hangman's post (Γ). Epsilon (ε) was a very vulnerable letter, a letter to feel sorry for because of its open half-circles, but a great addition that any word would be proud to have in its repertoire because epsilon looked so beautiful. Words with too many epsilons I felt sorry for, because they seemed steeped in vulnerability, like the word *eleos*, which means mercy. N was a sophisticated letter, naturally written tall, linear and elegant; it stands strong while joining what can never meet – two parallels. Capital theta (Θ) you had nothing to worry about, a self-sufficient letter, a closed circle with a dash in the middle, never lonely. Words with thetas seemed as independent as a military garrison.

Once I had learned the individual letters I practised writing sentences by copying selected passages from the Bible. My notebook was soon filled with quotes like, 'Judgements are prepared for scorners and stripes for the back of fools,' or, 'A foolish son is the calamity of his father.' She corrected me with admonitions in French. '*Ce n'est pas comme ça*,' or, '*Mais, non!*' After a few weeks of biblical instruction she opened a book of poetry by Cavafy. My task was to copy the poems. While I followed Cavafy's stanzas she would pause to tell me how polite he had been to her when they had met in Alexandria, a true gentleman who worked in an office of the Bureau of Irrigation Works by day and wrote poetry by night. As I wrote she recited the poem as if in front of an audience and when she was done there would be a satisfied stillness in the room that my imagination filled with applause. 'They don't make poets like him any more,' she would say and shut the book.

She taught me that Greek words might be funny. Fallen leaves make a *sousouro*, she said, when the wind rushes through them. Politicians who are full of themselves are *pompodis*. A car that's falling apart is a *saravalaki*. *Tzitziki* is the Greek word for cicada, a word that sounds like the insect's call. Some words were invented to sound like things. The word *laothalassa* literally meant a sea of people, an orgiastic multitude. The open alphas were like the crash of waves against the shore; in *lao* the mouth went from the open alpha to the rounded omicron and pronouncing it required disciplined effort, the energy of a crowd itself.

On her dresser, next to the fans which she used on hot days, my grandmother kept three icons of saints and, behind them, a crucifix with Christ's nearly naked body arched in that peculiar pose of pain and deliverance. Pictures of her Polish father hung from the wall, a man with a fierce beard, a monocle and an erect bearing. She told me he fought the Russians in Lithuania, was exiled in Siberia, escaped and joined some old *révolutionnaires* in Paris, trained in the Garibaldi school for rebels in Italy before joining the Greeks to liberate Ioannina from the Turks in 1871. There was also a large picture of my grandfather and my grandmother when they were young. It was only after weeks had gone by and I had stared at the pictures countless times that I suddenly realized that my grandfather and she had once lived under the same roof, inhabited the same bed and eaten their breakfast together.

'Why don't you live with *Pappou* any more?' I asked her one day while copying out 'The God Abandons Anthony'.

'We're divorced,' she replied and then pointed to the next stanza so I couldn't ask any more. Divorced since 1927, my mother told me, a period which belonged to the palaeolithic age for me, a remote world of model-T Fords and women with veils and people who walked too fast – like in the silent movies of that era. So it was with some excitement that I told her that *Pappou* would be visiting us for lunch one day.

When she heard the news she opened her anthology of poems. Yet rather than start reciting she deposited the book on her lap and from the window of her bedroom stared at slices of bark which hung from the trunks of the birch trees like empty shirt sleeves. After a long silence she began the lesson, but for the duration of the hour, as I sat hunched over her small desk, she barely paid attention to my writing and didn't guide me. Free of her vocal correctives and that solid grip over my fingers my writing degenerated into child-like scribbles, losing all traces of the adult-like beauty I thought was mine. My alphas were so small the open hole was filled with ink and my gammas barely crossed below the line. At some point she lifted her hand and scrutinized my sloppy work. I expected to hear her cries of '*Mais, non!*' but instead she patted my head absent-mindedly and said it was too hot a day for such hard work. We would continue tomorrow, she said, and stood to gather up the utensils.

The following day when I showed up for my lesson, she was sitting on her bed reading a letter. Hanging from the closet handle was a dark blue dress and beneath that were three pairs of shoes. Her open jewellery box held a mass of necklaces, thin and tiny, tangled up with each other. Her hearing-aid sat on the writing table, and, because she had her back to me, she couldn't know I had entered the room. When I stood close I saw over her shoulder the date at the top right corner of the letter: 6 December 1910. The words were larger than hers and swerved sideways, as if written in a rush, but none the less preserved the calligraphic principles she had taught me. This was a man's writing. Though I was tempted to read on, I was also embarrassed to cheat. When we played cards, I knew it was ridiculously easy to cheat on her, so for that very reason I didn't. I walked in front of her and stood there. When she saw me she immediately brought the letter close to her chest, then returned it to a wooden box which held similar letters of onion-skin paper. She told me she didn't remember that we'd put off yesterday's session for today, but soon enough we were bending over her desk. She held my hand with her coarse fingers. Her attention to my efforts was so slight that soon I was drawing alphas as big as a cat's head.

'What's this?' she said, pointing to a cat's head.

'But *you're* leading me,' I replied, 'it's not my fault.' She said nothing. '*Yiayia*, we can do our lessons afterwards.'

'Afterwards?'

'After *Pappou*.'

She stared at me as if she hadn't understood. Then she nodded her head. 'Yes, yes. After *Pappou*.'

Saturday morning, the day of my grandfather's arrival, and the house was on the move. Elvira had prepared a large meal of rice, chicken and béchamel sauce. My mother had promised us double pocket-money if we cleaned up our rooms by midday. My grandmother's door was shut all morning and except for the sound of water rushing through the tap in the washroom, there was nothing to indicate that she had even woken up for the morning. She never took breakfast anyway, but today no one had seen her.

Yet when we heard the rumble of cars outside our house and the small cavalcade of cop cars and motorcycles, her door opened and she stepped outside. She was dressed as if she was going to a soirée. A dark veil hid her face and her sleek blue skirt reached down to her ankles. With those fingers whose strength I had come to know well she clutched a small silver purse from which hung beads. She asked me to help her down the stairs and she followed me, placing one hand on my shoulder. I took each step like a kid, with care, joining one foot to the other before venturing down the next step.

When I reached the ground floor I saw my grandfather in the hallway. His maroon tie was decorated with white palm fronds that looked rather like the skeletons of fish. When he saw me he opened his arms to receive me but then his hands dropped to his sides. A cloud crossed his face, the smile vanished, and he turned instead to greet Lydia, Jason and Hector. My grandmother squeezed my shoulder hard, involuntarily I think, then released me and I heard her steps fading behind me. I ran to my grandfather and let him lift me into the air. When he put me down I raced towards the kitchen but she wasn't there. I knocked on the bathroom door, once, twice, turned the handle but it was locked. She didn't join us for lunch and nobody said anything when Elvira took her plate away. That brief meeting in the hallway was the last time my grandparents ever saw each other.

At our next lesson she asked me to read to her from something called *The Secrets of the Swamp*, by Penelope Delta: 640 action-packed pages about the exploits of a boy living on the border of Greece and Bulgaria during the war of 1905. Turning to page one I read this:

The sun, setting, reddened the snow-covered peaks of Olympus, goldened the waterholes left by yesterday's rain in muddy plains which stretched for ever, ashen, ugly, deserted.

'Ah, yes,' my grandmother said, nodding her head. 'Northern Greece.' She wore a woollen waistcoat and was knitting something. While I read I could hear the needles click against each other. Her glasses were perched on her nose so she could look up at me and down at her progress without a problem. She looked more grandmotherly than ever, nothing like the stylish lady she had dressed up as for my grandfather. The only thing missing was a rocking chair. I read a few more paragraphs.

'Penelope wanted to write a book in simple Greek,' my grandmother began, 'and she did it. We were friends of hers, your grandfather and I.' It seemed hard to believe that anybody could know someone whose name was on the cover of a school book but I didn't doubt my grandmother in anything. Whatever she said was the truth. 'Your grandfather wanted Greek to be understood by all people. He knew the language well, that one did.'

'Like in the letters?'

'Which letters?'

'The ones in your black box.'

'I know you saw me reading them,' she said. I nodded my head guiltily. 'Come early tomorrow,' she said.

Next day I found her sitting on her bed, a mass of crinkled onion-skin pages around her. Some were folded in half, some were small like from a notepad, others as big as two sheets together. Rather than gather them up and stuff them into the box like last time, she asked me to sit on the chair.

'One day,' she said, 'you will learn to cherish the shape of words. One day you will write love letters and you will win any woman's heart with the sheer neatness and power of your writing style.'

She handed me the letter. 'The first time I saw your grandfather,' she said, 'he was being held by *gendarmes*, who were taking him to jail. Years later, on one of our anniversaries, he wrote me this.'

Just like today, my Lydia, in 1907, remember, I was being taken in for the inquiry for the student troubles and I saw you on the steps of the Law School, with your white *chapeau*. We hadn't yet confessed. I blushed, you blushed, and these bright blushes lit my prison cell. And ever since then I have waited for you, just as I waited – how could I not? – for your letter in jail; what absolute relief to have received even one letter from you. Were you real? Were you false? Inside the prison I asked this question many times without being able to answer it.

The writing was like hers: imaginary horizontal lines appeared between each neat sentence; the smooth rightward tilt of letters, the curlicues for capitals, the upturned deltas and long tails that dipped beneath the imaginary horizontals.

She showed me a picture of the two of them together. In her eyes there is a sadness as if she knows one day she will be in a bedroom, alone, showing this picture to her grandson.

But she didn't let me see any more letters. 'You're too young,' was her excuse. A few months later she told me that my calligraphy was passable and that I could practise on my own. We were both sad that I wouldn't be joining her in the afternoon. The following year she took my younger brother under her tutelage and taught him some of the surprises of the Greek alphabet. But once, when we compared notes, I asked him about the sturdy lambdas and the vulnerable epsilons. He thought I was crazy. My grandmother didn't teach him that part.

A few years later, on a cold day in the suburb of King City, north of Toronto, while kids sharpened their skates and slapped hockey sticks against pucks and snowmobiles roared in the distance, we sat in front of the television and switched channels in the hope of finding news of my grandfather's funeral. We didn't know if they were going to show anything. My grandmother had been crossing herself ever since we learned of his death. Her face looked worn but in her eyes rather than sadness I saw a small bright light.

Then, on the six o'clock news, for a full minute, we saw footage of the crowd surrounding the coffin. A close-up showed my mother in a black scarf and sunglasses, my older brother and my sister – they had been given special permission to enter the country – being pushed by the crowd practically on to the hearse. Behind the Canadian commentator's words we could hear a roar and the slogan, 'Old Man of Democracy, rise up and see us! Rise up, Old Man!' An aerial shot showed hundreds of thousands walking slowly behind the funeral car. The crowds flooded into the First Cemetery of Athens and were backed up past Hadrian's Arch, reaching as far as the Greek parliament. Then the news flash was over and we sat there in silence.

My grandmother spoke first. Even in his last moments, she said, he managed to gather a real *laothalassa*. Her voice sounded harsh. It was the first hint I got of the real reason behind their separation. Politics. Not that I should have been surprised. She was the one who had told me that politics was the death of the family.

Once he was gone, she seemed eager to talk about him. She started to sing songs that he had sung to woo her, usually German songs, but some in French. She told us about Leipzig and Berlin before the First World War, and about the first time they held hands behind his father's church in Patras, and how he stole from her a breathless kiss inside the belfry. She told us how my grandfather had carried her through the streets of Chios one night, searching for a doctor, knocking on every door, shouting in the streets, until finally a midwife appeared to help with the baby and how my father was born in the middle of a garden, under a fig tree. Every year that went by, she said, every year that she grew older brought her that much closer to her husband.

We buried her in the same cemetery as my grandfather, though at quite a distance from each other. Her letters she left to us. For years I couldn't look at them. But one day as I read them, I recalled that brief moment in our home when their gaze met, the day she dressed in case he had changed his mind and wanted to speak to her.

January, 1909

I want to be the wind in your hair, the teardrop of your eye, the breath of your mouth, the smile of your lips, the tip of your tongue. I love you, I will love you, I have loved you.

March, 1910

So what if it was insane to meet on Tuesday next to the church; we quenched our thirst. My hungry lips, my burning heart, cooled. Joy doesn't walk streets, you must chase after it, beneath the table, before the theatre, in the drop of sunlight on your cheek.

When she taught me how to write, when I blew on the creamy sheet to dry the ink and pressed down hard with the blotter, she saw my grandfather in his military uniform drying the words he'd written for her over half a century ago:

August, 1924
From the moment of our parting in the streetcar your eyes live inside me, follow me everywhere. I left, my heart is wax, I return to you, my Lydia. I open the window to my office and let in a whirlwind of pain. Let's close the windows, the door, the voices of the world, let's be alone, alone. You and I.
    Receive my soul.

In one letter, when they are no longer living together, he asks her for a divorce. It's not that he doesn't love her, he wrote, it's that their marriage holds him back. Unlike the earlier ones, this one is free of his lazy rightward tilt; instead the words are upright and run across the page at neat right angles, perfectly horizontal, perhaps his most exquisite calligraphic effort. He wrote that his life required exhaustion in battle, whether in victory or in defeat. He was born when a crowd gathered in a square and died when it died. This passion, he said, he could share with nobody. He told her nothing of the famous actress who, along with four trunks of clothes and two poodles, would move in with him days after the divorce.

12   *The Kings of August*

One Sunday morning in early May when a sun as big as all of Canada rose above the corner of Ontario where we now lived, I put on my Adidas sneakers and grass-stained jeans to cut the lawn. Passing through the large den that led to the garage, I came across Hector, listening to a transistor radio our father had bought him at the duty-free in Hamburg. He was lying on the sheepskin rug and leaning his head against the Staetler polygraph used to print the bi-monthly resistance newsletter. Unlike me, Hector was going to let this Sunday go by as if he was already in retirement.

'For once,' I said to him, 'Just this once, can't *you* do the lawn?' Hector looked up at me and squinted. The sun streamed through the windows. Jason, who was in Boston and Lydia, who wasn't male, were naturally exempted from such chores.

'I don't think Dad can see the grass from Australia.'

'While Dad is giving speeches we can at least do a few chores here.'

'I want to listen to Monty Python.' He turned the volume up. His blond hair smelled of shampoo, his skin was fresh and clean, his eyes were green-blue, his nose slightly upturned. He possessed something of my father's charm and my mother's good looks. Perhaps it was this I couldn't forgive.

'Have you seen the lawn lately? C'mon, take a look.' To sound convincing I had to get myself angry. With his loose and jaunty step he made his way over to the window and brought his hand to his eyes as if trying hard to see.

'Holy cow, the grass is high as my ankle! Time to call in the Royal Mounted Lawn Police before we choke in it!' With that bright light burning in his eyes, he looked up at me, smiled, then flopped down on the white *flokati* rug.

'How can you listen to the radio while people are in jail?' With a grand gesture I pointed to the poster-filled wall. One showed a tank inside the Parthenon. Another showed a black fist clutched in agony. There was an ad for a concert: 'Pete Seeger and Joan Baez join Melina Mercouri to sing freedom songs for Greece. New York, 1968.' An American flag had fifty skull and crossbones instead of stars, and the red stripes were runny, like blood.

'Ugh. Jacky Almond has this Raquel Welch poster from a movie about cavemen a million years ago.' I knew the poster he was referring to. Raquel was dressed in a skin bikini, and stood in the sand with her legs half-spread as if she were braced for some neanderthal to tackle her. For a moment both Hector and I were lost in Raquel's arms. But she belonged over there, to another home.

'Forget her. You think every kid who's thirteen owns a radio?'

'No, only some kids.'

I reached down and turned the radio off. I was stronger than him and we both knew he couldn't beat me in a fight.

'I think, instead of Monty Python, I'll read *Batman*.' He rolled over on his back and held up a comic-book.

'What will happen,' I continued, 'if there's a third world war and your radio doesn't work any more?'

'Leave me alone.'

I tore the comic book from his hands and threw it away. It sailed up and came down on the leather couch. Hector stared up at the ceiling, hands holding an invisible book.

'Why do you think I don't have a radio?' I stood right over his head. Maybe because I'd just seen the movie *Yellow Submarine*, from upside down his chin looked like his forehead and his nostrils like eyes. I guess I looked the same to him. 'You won't be able to survive when we become poor. Think for a moment, what if we have to give everything away, what if we finally have socialism? What if there's a dictatorship in Canada, too?'

'Holy Majoly. Can't you leave me alone? Christ!'

I left the den, letting the screen door slam behind me. For once I wanted to see the lawn neat without me having to cut it. Since the night of the coup, on a regular basis, I had nightmares of the fanatic officer shooting me in the head and I attended my funeral at least twice a month – where I noted who in my family was crying and who wasn't – but the sight of a neat lawn and trim bushes relieved me of my conviction that adulthood meant chaos and disorder. Hector had no such compunctions.

I dragged the lawn-mower out of the dark garage and brought it to a thicket of tall grass. It had rained the night before and the grass glistened. Wet grass was difficult to cut – you weren't supposed to touch it, and it usually caused the lawn-mower to choke up – but I was determined to finish the job, rain or no rain.

At full throttle – to make sure Hector could hear it – the lawn-mower turned the grass into mulch. In front of the Procrustean blades, bugs and tiny flying things with unknown names leapt out of harm's way. A shiny, bright-green frog, limbs extended, bounced beautifully over the body of the lawn-mower and escaped into another thicket of grass. When I was done, I surveyed the results with satisfaction, then dragged the lawn-mower to another unruly patch. Getting there I slipped. My hands went up into the air for balance and, instead of letting go, I pulled the lawn-mower up towards me, right over my foot.

I left the Newmarket emergency ward the following day in a wheelchair, my bandaged foot up in the air like a flag. I had vague images of a surgeon sliding a small saw back and forth over my foot for a few minutes. The grate of its metal teeth reached right up to my chest.

I refused to look at the damage. I wore a thick woollen sock which I didn't remove even in the shower. I knew something was missing but not exactly what and how much. There were times when it seemed I had no choice, that my foot would come into viewing range – like when changing my water-soaked sock – but I always turned my head at the last moment. I told myself that the accident happened so that my charred remains would be more easily identifiable in the aftermath of a war or the grenade thrown at my father by Greek fanatics.

While I recuperated – I was supposed to remain in a wheelchair for the month of June and stand five minutes each hour – Hector spent time with his friends. I could no longer be his partner. He would dash out of the front door with a quick, 'Bye!' and when he returned at the end of the day, he was sweaty, his face was darkened from the sun, his corduroys were soiled from the humus of the dank forests, his socks were full of burrs, and he smelled of trees. While Hector was out, I watched the person our father had hired to do the lawn – a man named McNeal who smoked a cigar and had a face like moths had chewed it – make his slow and lazy progress across my old kingdom. Thanks to me, Hector was for ever freed from such duties.

Hector gave me a butterfly which he'd caught with Jacky Almond. He told me they chased it for over two hours; it had an erratic flight pattern – just when you thought it was going to turn left it turned right, just when you thought it was slowing down to land on the underside of a maple leaf or on the trunk of a birch tree it flew over your head and you had to backtrack to keep up. I pretended to like it. It was an orange-brown Buckeye, a rare butterfly in these parts, with purple and blue eyespots on each wing.

I took a match to its wings and watched it burn. It gave off a strong, smoky odour, like burning hair. Hector didn't try to stop me. My foot made me invincible.

'This is what I think of your present,' I said. All that was left was this diaphanous frame of wing and a body that looked like McNeal's cigar ash. After that Hector didn't bother to say goodbye when he left the house.

His second mistake was offering me his radio, which I took gladly. I ripped out the wires connecting the batteries, and returned it to him.

'So you can listen to Monty Python,' I said.

One night as he slept, I limped on crutches into his bedroom, stuck my foot with the woollen sock in front of his face, then turned on the light. He woke up and banged his head against my ankle.

'How do you like them apples?' I said in a low voice. This was the closest to pure evil I had ever come. Hector pushed his body as far back against the wall as he could. There was fear in his eyes. He looked pale and helpless in his loose pajamas. I switched off the light, said 'Goodnight,' and hopped away. I slept soundly that night, without any of my usual nightmares about the dictatorship.

It was as if I had handed my dreams to him.

He began to hyperventilate at night. From my room I listened to him take deep long breaths, and then shorter and shorter ones until he sounded like a dog panting. My father was off on one of his anti-Junta North American speaking tours and I heard my mother tell him over the phone that for the past week Hector 'was sinking into an embrace of deep silences'. Shapes floated through his mind, a flaming red pyramid inside a bright yellow cube, complicated geometres with convexities and hollows and spiralling things like the turns of a screw, springs, and objects with lots of holes. Sort of like a lawnmower blasted apart by a ray gun. Sort of like the dreams I should have been having.

They sent him to a 'specialist'. A good soldier, Hector had told my mother nothing about my behaviour. She explained to me and Lydia that my accident had reminded Hector of the night of the dictatorship when the soldiers had pointed guns at us and beaten up our father in front of him. My accident had triggered something dormant in his 'psyche'.

When he returned from his speaking tour, my father made a point of coming home early from the university and spending the evening in Hector's bedroom; he spoke to him in this gentle, sing-song voice that carried into my room and lulled me to sleep, too. I had never seen this side of my father. I wasn't seeing it now, either. Hector was. I didn't want to remind myself that my father had come to my room only once after my accident.

One morning I woke up with the belief that since I had gotten Hector into this state, I could also get him out of it. I tried to undo my punishment but like a minor god whose powers are spent, I couldn't. I bought him a new radio, but, after clicking it on and off a few times and turning up the volume, he slipped it into his desk drawer. From the Richmond Hill pet shop I ordered two butterflies, a Tiger Swallowtail and a Mourning Cloak, but when they arrived, he stashed them with barely a glance in the same drawer.

By the end of July I was taking short walks into the forest where nobody could see how I propelled myself. My mother would drive me to an isolated spot and I would hobble into the brush, leaving the crutches in the back seat. She reassured me that in no time I would be back to normal and that come spring I could even play basketball. When I got tired I leaned against a tree, or if I slipped, I grabbed a branch hanging above me, or if I was really in pain, I simply lay down on the thick mattress of dead leaves and thrust my leg into the sky like a mast.

Once, sitting on the gnarled roots of an old tree, a long-legged deer with graceful and dignified movements came within yards of where I was sitting. I held my breath, afraid to make the slightest sound, and watched until the deer ran off into the bush, flashing me its bushy tail. I was so excited that as soon as I came home I limped into Hector's room and, in urgent tones, told him what I'd seen. He listened to me, the first time since he'd stopped speaking to me. From then on I made sure I told him about each day's events: the eagle circling above for hours, the groundhog that dipped its snout into the moist thick dirt and stared at me dumbly, and the porcupine that waddled into a stream and stayed there as if it was waiting for something to happen. I brought him apples from the Schwartzes' orchard and wild strawberries from the plains between the forests.

One sunny August morning, nearly three months after my accident, he followed me out of the house but at a good distance. For Hector's sake I tried to walk without limping. When the throbbing grew too strong, I would take a pit-stop but pretended there were other reasons – like a leaf or a flower or a bird fluttering in the brush. When I stopped to study an insect on the trunk of a tree he caught up with me and stared.

'Weird,' he said.

'Yeah,' I said casually, for this was the first time since his hyperventilating that he'd said a word to me. 'Look. One pine-needle is the body, the other four are its legs.' Hector touched it with a stick. The insect dropped a few inches and dangled in the air from what looked like a thin web. The insect was playing dead. Finally it scrambled up the trunk, away from our reach, moving like five skinny sticks. We wandered even deeper into the forest. Hector lopped off yellow and orange fungus from tree trunks with cries of joy. 'Hup!' he shouted and karate-chopped a bright chunk of fungus. 'Haee-hay!' He kicked over the large mushrooms and I would squat as if to examine their dark and spoke-like undersides, an excuse to relieve my pounding foot. I think we stayed out in the forest for over two hours. When we returned my foot throbbed and ached but Hector's face glowed.

My parents encouraged our treks. My father said I was a living example of what economists called 'externalities'. My walks were not only good for my foot but also served to relieve Hector's overwhelming anxiety. That's the way a socialist economy was supposed to work, he said, through co-operation and mutual benefit. Only my father could have turned our walks through the forests of Ontario into a lesson in political economy.

For the rest of August we went out into the forest every day. One morning we were lying down in an open field with stalks of wild grass around us, staring up at the sky. I asked him to tell me the first thing he thought of when our father told us after his release from jail that we were leaving Greece and moving to Canada.

'The first thing?' Hector closed his eyes. 'Whiteness. Igloos. Cubes of ice. Snow. Lots of snow.'

'Canada sucks!'

'Really sucks!' he echoed.

Neither Hector nor I wanted to admit it, but Canada seemed as great as Greece. Maybe even greater, which was why we started to say things like, 'Canada is for the birds,' or, 'Canada sucks.' Too much enthusiasm for our land of exile felt like a betrayal of Greece, a betrayal of our father, who was travelling around the world for the 'cause'.

I tore some stems of grass and showed Hector how to bite the end of them.

'It's like a squirt of juice,' I said. We chewed on grass stems.

'Did you ever expect animals and forests?'

'No.' He looked at my foot and grew quiet.

'Look,' I said, 'like mom said, the dictatorship in Greece was like a country having one big accident. That's a lot worse than what happened to me. Anyway, this here,' I said and looked at my foot, 'this here was all my fault. You got that? It really was. I mean it.' He nodded his head, but didn't look at me.

The next day we went into the forest and found a team of men cutting down trees and clearing the land to make way for an extension of Route 13. Hector and I sat on a large sawn-off stump whose frayed edge pinched our behinds. Men strapped chains across dead tree trunks so tractors could tear them loose and drag them into a fire which was kept alive by slow-burning tyres. Soon our clothes and hair smelled of burning rubber. A mechanical arm from the back of a huge truck reached out and clamped on to a tree, tore it right out of the ground so the roots dangled there, and, while clumps of damp earth rained down, a sharp ring ran up the length of the tree and snapped off its branches like grapes. A light burned in Hector's eyes as the naked trunk was then fed into the mouth of another machine which shredded it into sawdust with a great shriek. Here were things that spun and yawed, that sliced and crunched. Bits of wood floated around us.

I winced with each cry of the machines and my foot throbbed as if it knew that dangers lurked nearby, but I didn't want Hector to sense that any of this bothered me. I told him that this was all part of 'capitalism's orgies', as our father put it. Wise, glad to be let in on an older brother's knowledge, he nodded his head like an adult. 'Orgies,' he repeated. While we spoke, we watched two men chop down a tree and the pain in my foot grew so great that I couldn't ignore it any longer.

'Hector,' I said, getting up suddenly, 'let's go.'

I hobbled into the thicket and this time I made no effort to hide my limp. I came to an opening in the forest lit by shafts of light streaming through the canopy, a place free of all man's careful symmetries. Caught up in the wondrous glitter of dust, made visible by the brightness of the sun's rays, I accidentally banged my foot hard against a root hidden beneath layers and layers of dead leaves. The pain shot through my leg. I lay down, unable to move, eyes shut. I visualized the accident all over again, the frightened frog, the thick grass over the drain, Lydia's cries, Hector holding the radio in the doorway with tears in his eyes and my mother driving wildly through the narrow streets of Newmarket.

'Hector,' I said, trying to get up. 'It's like a million needles.'

He pushed his hair out of his eyes. 'You're not going to take your shoe off, are you?' His fear was at least as great as mine.

'Why don't you cover your eyes?' I undid the shoelace, pulled the tongue back and stretched the shoe wide and removed it gently. The thick sock hid the strange shape of my foot. I pulled the sock half-way down and massaged the arch, while the sock, sliding softly back and forth, soothed the area I refused to touch. Hector removed his hands from his face and stared hard. Suddenly, as if his stare had something to do with it, the sock slipped off. The exposed foot dangled in the air like a strange creature.

Hector clenched and unclenched his fists. 'Gross,' he said in a whisper. He flipped his hair back and forth but didn't take his eyes off it.

'Really gross,' I repeated, leaning this way and that to take it in from all angles. Three round rings, like the eyespots on the Buckeye butterfly wings, indicated the absent toes. I leaned over and counted each and every stitch.

'Twenty-eight,' I said and looked up at him.

'Holy cow,' he said. His face was bright. There was pride in his voice.

Some time after that, Hector stopped seeing shapes in his dreams and no longer hyperventilated at night. We started to spend our Sundays together like two men in retirement, listening to Monty Python, playing Chinese chequers and reading comic-books. But sometimes I wouldn't play at all. I'd stand at the window and check out the height of the grass. When McNeal was a couple of days late and the unruly grass provoked my terrible compulsion for neatness, when the desire to put everything into perfect order became overwhelming, that's when I wished that once, just once, I had managed to get Hector to cut the lawn.

13   *Silent Descent*

The first dead body I ever saw was that of an old man. He lay on the beach of Rafina with bits of seaweed stuck to his legs and the chain of his crucifix tangled around one ear. Next to him a young man rocked on his knees and shouted, 'It's my fault! It's all my fault!' and threw sand into the air. 'If I'd only pulled him out sooner!' He hit his forehead with his palm and nobody stopped him or said a kind word to him. We just watched, the lot of us, the children and the men and the women gathered there. I was relieved that something so tangible as the young man was to blame for his death.

My second dead man came a few years later. My father called me into his office and told me that he couldn't attend the funeral of a political colleague. He wanted me to go instead. So far I'd been a godfather (*nonos*) three times, best man (*koumbaros*) once, second best man (*parakoumbaros*) twice, and now he wanted me to become a funeral eulogist. I told him I couldn't go because I had basketball practice, lots of homework, important chores, and that I suffered from seven different kinds of sleeplessness. He raised his eyebrows.

'Why me?' I asked. 'What's wrong with Lydia or Jason?'

'You're the only one who knows Vassili.' My father searched through his papers. 'There's a picture of him somewhere . . . where is it now . . .' I could see its edge sticking out beneath a book. He searched a little while longer but only succeeded in covering it up completely.

'Anyway,' he said, finally giving up. 'Vassili Regouko. You know him.'

'That's a goofy name, Regouko.'

My father told me that he was the one who spoke with that strong accent I liked to imitate, who said *Bastin* instead of Boston, *sunupapits* instead of son of a bitch and *kupacaffee*. I shook my head. 'Remember?' I fought away a vague image of a man with a moustache and bright white teeth who laughed at my jokes over dinner last year.

'OK. OK. I guess I do.'

My father clapped his hands once and stood. 'Good,' he said. Now that that was settled, I needed to know only a few things: that Vassili had been a poor farmer who emigrated to the States from Larissa, that he owned one of the best Greek diners in Skokie, had arranged successful marriages for all three of his sisters and was well-liked by the Greek community in Chicago. He died of a heart attack in his garage while making – believe it or not – a protest placard against the dictatorship.

On the flight from Toronto I read and re-read the small note my father had written for the funeral, glad I didn't have to learn it by heart. I decided I would read it fast, keep my eyes pinned to the paper and avoid looking at the open casket. 'Don't worry,' my father had told me when he dropped me off at the airport, 'it'll be over fast.' That's what the dentist always said.

A ball of darkness greeted me at O'Hare airport. Skirts, stockings, armbands, ties, all black. I did my best to give off an air of dignified sadness. I stood straight, shook hands slowly, spoke in low, respectful tones and avoided long sentences because excessive garrulousness on my part was a sign of too much life and too much life seemed rather blasphemous at a time like this.

Sotiri, a nervous man in a woollen turtle-neck and a leather jacket like the kind my father now wore, pumped my hand vigorously. He squeezed his cigarette hard between his fingers as if it might suddenly jump from his hands like a living thing. 'It's an honour for the Regoukos family,' he said, 'an honour.'

The dead man's wife hugged me and expressed her gratitude. The mother, with a veil over her grey-white hair, cried and kissed me over and over. 'Enough,' Sotiri said impatiently. 'Mother, enough!' Two kids in dark blue suits and black ties gave me their little hands, heads erect. I didn't feel the least desire to touch, hug or kiss. This was *their* dead man, not mine.

In the back seat of a sleek limousine the wife looked up at me. 'Vassili told us about you,' she said. 'He said you laughed at all of his jokes.' I nodded my head and didn't tell her that it wasn't me but Vassili who had laughed at *my* jokes. The two children sat on the limo's fold-out seats and stared at me. The mother began to sing and I made out some words in Greek: 'Earth for a blanket, rock for a pillow, small pebbles for a brother and sister.'

'Mother,' Sotiri said, 'please.' Her low deep tones grew

into a sonorous eastern-sounding melody and finished on a single shrill, drawn-out note, a needle in our ears. 'Mother!' Sotiri banged the seat with his fist, looked at me and then shrugged his shoulders. She wouldn't stop. I cracked my knuckles and stared at the floor. 'Soon you marry the black earth and I the black clothes.'

At the entrance of the Greek Orthodox cemetery an old man got up from his wooden stool and waited for our limo to stop. He bent down and hung his large hands over the driver's half-open window in a comfortable, lazy fashion. 'There are two today,' he said in Greek. 'What is the unfortunate soul's name?' Regouko, I thought. Gook-o Regouko. Goofy Gooko. The two boys stared at me so intently I thought they had heard my thoughts and I looked out of the window.

The cemetery was filled with elaborate tombstones. One was built like a miniature Acropolis and another showed Hercules carrying a dead man on his shoulders. An imposing guardian angel with long hair and wings that curved high above his shoulders stood over the figure of a sleeping girl. One hand hovered protectively above her head while the index finger of his other hand touched his lips. *Shhhh*. We came to a halt and got out of the cars; doors slammed shut and gravel crunched underfoot.

Placed between Sotiri and the wife, I started walking while the rest followed behind at a short but respectful distance. I noticed my shoelace was undone and without a thought crouched down. My face grew hot when I realized that the whole cortège waited while I did up my shoe. I finished as fast as I could and we proceeded in formation until we reached a small roofless temple, open on two sides. Sotiri took my hand and led me around the shining coffin which lay on a squat marble table. The wife, the mother, Sotiri, the two kids, the priest and I now stood on one side of the coffin while the small group of relatives stood on the other. The men removed their hats, the women folded their hands in front of them and everybody stopped shuffling and whispering until it was very quiet. In the distance I saw the elevated highway and I imagined the rush of cars speeding toward O'Hare and I tried to convince myself that the funeral would be over fast.

The priest kissed his crucifix and began to intone something in a long nasal drone, while two short psalmists in grey suits seconded his phrases. The priest finished his short recitation with a resounding *Defte telefteon aspasmon!* – 'Proceed to the last embrace!' and then, without the slightest hesitation, he walked up to the casket and flung open the lid. There was a moment of silence like the kind that occurs when a performance has finished abruptly, just before the outburst of applause.

'Vassili!' shouted the wife, leaning into the coffin. 'Why did you do this to us?' From where I stood all I could see was the plush white interior of the lid.

'Vassili!' Sotiri shouted. 'How could you have left us so soon?' He lifted his hands into the air. 'You will never grow bent and wrinkled like some of us, you will remain for ever strong!'

'Why?' the mother cried, stepping up to the casket. 'Why?' Then she slapped her forehead with her hands and fell to her knees.

Holding my breath, I too stepped up so I could peer into the coffin. Manoli had once told me that the price the living had to pay for remaining alive was to look directly at the dead man's face. His cheeks were blue-green and his lips were thin and purple. Maybe he did say *Bastin* instead of Boston and *Tsikago* instead of Chicago, but I didn't remember him. I let out my breath and stepped back.

An old man with eyes like wet raisins hobbled up to the coffin, grabbed hold of it and tried to shake it, rocking back and forth with his tiny body.

'Vassili!' he rasped. 'What do you see in there? Tell us, what do you see?'

The priest leaned over. 'Speak,' he whispered into my ear, 'speak quickly before they go too far.'

I retrieved my father's note from my jacket and held it up for all to see. The crying faded to whimpers and whispers. Mother and wife sobbed in each other's arms while Sotiri comforted them both.

'This is from my father,' I said loudly. My hands shook. The old man looked at me as if I were about to answer his questions.

'A man lies here today,' I began, 'a man who fought for democracy.' Already I felt better.

'A boy!' the mother cried out. 'He was my little boy!'

A brawny man with a resonant voice came forward, leaned over, and kissed Vassili. 'He lives!'

'A man who fought for the release of Greece from the stranglehold of dictators,' I continued, 'a man who gave his life for the cause of . . .'

'You!' shouted the mother, pointing at me. 'Bring him back!' She rushed over and hugged me so hard that the paper got scrunched against my face while my arms were trapped between her breasts and my neck. She smelled like cabbage soup.

Sotiri pulled at her but she held tight. Then she released me and, before anybody could stop her, she jumped into the coffin. I almost expected that the man's face would swell and bloat with all that sudden weight on him but it remained rigid and expressionless. She passed her hands through his hair and caressed his forehead.

'Bring him back!' she shouted as she was lifted out of the coffin. Her eyes were smudged with make-up and a bubble of snot swelled beneath her nose.

'Read,' the priest commanded, 'read, for God's sake!'

When I was done six men wearing gloves approached the coffin and lifted it up and on to their shoulders. By the time we arrived at the burial site, the priest was already there, waiting patiently, Bible open. He glanced at his watch. The two kids stared at me as the coffin was lowered into the grave and stared while the screaming and crying rose into the sky, they stared at me even while the priest performed the final dust-to-dust, ashes-to-ashes part. To them it was very obvious who was to blame for their father's death.

Flowers landed soundlessly on the coffin but were crushed by the earth shovelled in by two diggers. The casket soon disappeared beneath a layer of dirt and at that very moment I thought I heard, descending all around me like the hiss of rain, a long-drawn-out *shhh*.

14 *On Use Values and Exchange Values*

My father needed someone to drive with him from Toronto to New York, where he was going to speak at a Greek–American fundraiser at Crystal Palace in Queens, Astoria, so he asked me to come along. On the way to New York we stopped to see the Niagara Falls from the Canadian side and, three hours later, once we were let into the States, we saw it from the American side. We agreed the Canadian side was more dramatic. We were detained at the border so the customs men could check my father's gun licence. The State Department had put him on some special 'harassment' list which meant that every time his name popped up on the computer they were supposed to make life difficult for him. That was one of the things I liked about my father – he was important enough to be on a computer list across the North Americas, a modern-day Pancho Villa, and yet he didn't seem particularly dangerous, except if you really knew him. He wore jeans without back pockets, Hush Puppies and a tweed jacket, and didn't look at all like someone who was leading a whole movement. But he was. And that he carried a gun was, for me, proof enough.

While four men searched the old Mercedes I continued a complicated calculation I'd begun outside Toronto, namely: how much was I worth – on a pure cost basis? What did it cost to reproduce someone like me? In one of my father's books I'd read about the minimum necessary social value needed to reproduce a human being. I began at the beginning, starting with Gerber baby food, nappies, baby-sitters, and went all the way up to the basketball sneakers now on my feet. When the agent finally let us through – muttering something about how the United States had too much democracy – I had reached the fifty-thousand-dollar mark. I was expensive.

Though we were now running late, my father was hungry, so we stopped outside Buffalo for lunch at a diner that had for a tourist attraction a small pond in the shape of the map of New York State and coffee brewed with water from the Niagara Falls. Purple dragon-flies and large water-beetles skimmed along the pond's dirty brown surface. A waitress wearing a tight polyester skirt, an apron, and a cap with her name on it, Estelle, showed us to our seats at one of the grey-flecked Formica tables with aluminium edges. We slid into the booth and my father brought out his meerschaum pipe, a box of Erinmore tobacco, two pipe-cleaners, and a silver-coloured Ronson lighter. Against all rules of gravity, the flame from his lighter dipped upside down into the bed of tobacco as he sucked hard. He repeated this action often, I think as a favour to me.

No one here would have known that we were rushing to get to New York City, nor that my father had once practically run a whole country, spoken to crowds that could fill two football fields, and was the leader of a worldwide network of forty-something, hard-smoking, hard-working, hyphenated Greeks who believed in the 'cause'. Nobody except my father, who I thought cared only about that, and me, who, because I thought he cared only about that, cared only about that too – after all, that was what it took to be a good follower: to know what your leader was thinking.

A man at the counter wore his trousers so low that some of the rear of his rear end showed. A large fly buzzed stubbornly against the glass dome covering a dry-looking slice of choc-olate cake, banging itself repeatedly against the invisible wall and finally found solace hovering above the hard-hat's ex-posed behind. Estelle brought the cheeseburgers with a side order of pickles and thick ruffled French fries, on plates so large they covered up half the table. At home my mother forbade this kind of food and for a moment I felt we were both part of the same conspiracy against my mother's injunc-tions, until my father thanked Estelle for 'her excellence and her delightful speed in procuring our sumptuous-looking lunch', and then smiled at her. I felt my face grow hot and expected Estelle to stare at him like he was an escapee from the Niagara Home for Emeritus Professors. Instead she brought her hand to her mouth and laughed and her body shook a little, enough so that I noticed parts of her body not obvious at first glance. Walking away from our table, she gave him an over-the-shoulder glance that I had seen only in the movies. He looked at her with this saucy, self-confident gaze, as if he'd just won an Oscar for best male actor.

Once we were done with the chewing and swallowing, my

father leaned back and laid one arm across the length of the booth as if he owned the place. I saw the bulge of the revolver from under his armpit. I leaned over the table.

'Shouldn't you be more careful?'

'Oh,' my father replied, 'you mean this,' and he opened his jacket for me and exposed, for a brilliant moment, the gleaming butt of his revolver, snug as a bug inside its brown leather holster. He wore one of those holsters that strap around your shoulders like a male brassière, the kind Steve McQueen wore in the movie *Bullitt*.

'Da-ad,' I said, looking around to make sure nobody had seen us. He adjusted his tweed jacket with an annoyed twitch of his shoulders, lifted his hand lazily into the air to command Estelle's attention and when she looked at us he scribbled in the air with an imaginary pen.

Instead of the bill and Estelle, the owner himself showed up, a man named Gus Antoniou, who had a red spot like the map of Albania on his forehead. Gus had recognized my father – he had voted for my grandfather in 1963 before emigrating to the States – and came over to tell us lunch was on him. My father slid out of the booth, stood, and with a genuine smile – to be recognized in such a place! – he patted Gus's back and told him what a great lunch it was and that the cheeseburger was a perfect medium-rare. If someone was watching them from afar, it was instantly clear that the man with the pipe, for all his awkward rumpledness and knobbly good-natured movements, was being fawned over by the more pert and alert, well-dressed and sleek-looking owner who was staring around at the few patrons with evident pride, as if he were talking to Frank Sinatra. My heart swelled and I felt cocky as if some of this Sinatra recognition belonged to me.

Gus gestured to a sad-looking creature behind the counter – his daughter Penelope, who, according to Gus, besides cooking our burgers, attended the Greek school in Buffalo each Sunday and had won the St George's Orthodox Church contest for best hand-woven island pillow. Gus himself had been recently elected chairman of the Church Parking Lot Committee. Penelope came close and offered us a menu.

'Will you sign it for us?' She spoke with her father's nasal twang and ran the words together. Instead of letting them know he was in a rush, he nodded and with a grand gesture drew his silver fountain pen from inside his jacket pocket. For a moment I wondered if he was going to 'accidentally' let the gun show, but he didn't. He sat down, put the menu in front of him, waved the pen like a dragon-fly skimming the surface of the pond, and brought the nib to rest. The blue ink spread while he thought of the dedication.

Gus leaned his large chin over my father's shoulder and watched him swish his name gracefully across the top of the menu. His handwriting was even and neat. My father rose from the table, slid a twenty under the plate – which Gus instantly snapped up and promised to frame – gathered up the pipes and cleaners and remaining accoutrements with those dignified movements of his, dropped the items into his jacket pocket, which was darkened at the edges from just such smoky company, tugged his jacket over his shoulders, shook Penelope's and her father's hands, said something about making it to New York on time, and with only a glance at me, walked hurriedly past the booths with their identical sugar-pourers and place-mats extolling the greater Buffalo area, but not before bending his head slightly at Estelle, who was holding the door open for him. Gus followed him to his car. Suddenly he was gone and I was still here.

I got up so fast I nearly spilled the glasses on our table, I overturned the salt-shaker – which I righted instantly – and then, squeezing my way along the booth at that awkward angle you have to adopt to slide out, legs wedged between the edge of the seat and the edge of the table, I lost my balance and had to sit down again. When I made it out, Penelope blocked the way. She brought her face close to mine and I looked down. Her toes curled inside her soft leather shoes. Ever since my lawn-mower accident I was jealous of anybody who still had all their toes.

'Can I have your signature, too?'

'What?' I said. 'Mine?' She nodded her head and smiled.

My cheek burned as if she'd kissed me. This was a gift, but not one I thought was undeserved. Maybe my signature didn't count for as much and would only get one tenth my father's value at an auction, but it carried some weight, did it not?

Through the window I saw the white Mercedes pull out of its parking space. I grabbed the menu, sat down again and realized I had no pen. 'This time, Alex,' my father had said the night before we left Toronto, 'the dictators can't survive the student protests.' It wouldn't do for him, the Pan-Hellenic Liberator, to be stuck in a place like Gus's diner in Buffalo while the colonels who ran Greece tendered their resignations to the international community. But it would be impolite to refuse Penelope's request. If he complained that I had delayed the trip, I would reply rather innocently that I was only following his own precepts concerning proper etiquette.

Sensing my father's brooding impatience, Penelope raced frantically through the restaurant in search of a blue-ink pen, since the red ones they used for taking orders were bad luck according to Gus. Breathing heavily, her face a deep shade of red, she thrust a chewed-up Bic pen in front of me; the three of us eagerly bent over the menu to watch me sign my name just below my father's message about Greek hearts across the North Americas 'struggling against the dictators'. I recalled something my grandmother had told me, that small letters were the sign of a small man and, though under the duress of a Mercedes horn emitting one long, excruciating honk, I knew I should show prescience. One day someone might decide to do a biography of my life and trace back all my memorabilia. When I finished, my surname was big and tall as one of the hamburger pictures on the menu.

I ran out of the door. He was leaning against the wheel with his chin on his hands like a model posing for a magazine. I raced around the front of the car, straightening the Mercedes symbol which I suddenly noticed was tilted backwards, plopped myself into the passenger seat and slammed the door.

'Go, go, go!' I shouted giddily to my father, as if we'd just robbed a bank. Gravel shot out from the back tyres and I imagined Gus and Penelope staring from the restaurant, shaking their heads, thinking that the two of us were on a mission to save the world.

Now we were alone again.

He turned and looked at me like a wolf with its head between its paws, eyes narrowing, ready to pounce, no longer the pipe-smoking professor but the leader on the podium raging against my injustice.

'No son of *mine* makes me wait and no son of *mine* gives *me* orders,' he said. His hand left the steering wheel. I heard a thwack – a punch more than a slap. I grew dizzy. Instinctively I scrunched myself up against the door and got as far away from him as I could. I sensed a familiar pain where his ring had dug into my cheekbone. His rage was like the wind in the Aegean: one moment calm as the still sea and the next moment rising to the force of a gale.

When tears stung my eyes I looked away and stared out at the gravel-laden shoulder which was strewn with slices of inner-tubing and bits of fan belts. We passed a hitch-hiker with hair down to his waist and a suntanned face. His cardboard sign read MUST U. MASS OR MY ASS IS GRASS. A smoke-stack with NIAGARA POWER CO written in faded blue smudged the sky with a purple haze. In the sunshade mirror I watched a welt rise up below my eye.

'Isn't capitalism awful?' I said.

'You think so, do you?' he said, gripping the wheel hard. 'Well, mister,' he said and his voice rose, 'without "capitalist" electricity you couldn't listen to your stereo or watch the Maple Leafs on television or make toast for breakfast.'

'But you're the one who . . .'

'Yes, I'm the one who tells you about assembly lines, child-labour and alienation.' He honked at the car in front of us to get out of the way, a sleek Dodge Charger with a jacked-up rear, exposing parts of its machinery and black radials. 'Capitalist by day and a rebel by night, that's what I am all right!' Then, realizing he'd said something that rhymed, he laughed. 'Ha!'

I wondered if this had something to do with Estelle, the waitress at the diner. He honked again, ramming his palm against the horn, and passed the Dodge. I slid down the seat as we passed and my pants came up to my waist. I had just read a science-fiction story where all cars were equipped with machine-guns, grenade launchers and ejection units that sent out tyre-puncturing metal flak, with hoses that shot out jets of oil, and knives that stuck out of the hub-caps like the scythes in Ben Hur. In the mirror I saw four guys in the Dodge Charger, their mouths and lips moving fast, forming enough F-words to fill a whorehouse. The two in the back were hunched over the front seat, their arms dangling like vines, and one of them, who looked like the fanatic that had tried to run me over when I was a kid living in Greece, poked his hand out of the window and gave us the finger. This was not the kind of car you honked at, even if you were the Pan-Hellenic Liberator.

'Dad, Holy Christ!' The speedometer was a thick brush of colour that rose vertically from the zero point and changed colours at every thirty-mile increase in speed. It now changed from green to green-and-red stripes and then when it rose past the hundred-mile mark it became deep red, a warning he ignored. When we reached a hundred and fifteen the old Mercedes was shaking. The door handle quivered and the glove-compartment door suddenly dropped open. The two-lane highway stretched out in front of us like the Arizona flats, and I thought we were about ready for lift-off.

Just outside Syracuse we pulled into one of those rest areas, those patches of asphalt and green that hang at the side of the highway like half-moons. In front of the imitation log-cabin toilet stood a vending machine. Patches of oil stained the asphalt, and scattered across the parking area were rings, bolts, gaskets and shards of glittering glass. A thicket of maples, underbrush and tall grass hid us from the highway, which was why this was a perfect place for the Dodge Charger to ambush us. I imagined it racing into the rest area with shotguns sticking out of its windows like cockroach antennae.

My father got out, stretched his arms, walked into the middle of the parking area and started to do some strange exercises he probably learned as a child growing up in Greece, and then ambled slowly over to the log-cabin toilet. When my father emerged I was hard at work, squatting next to the tyre, using his Ronson lighter to burn away a sheet of plastic that was caught in the axle. Bits of dust from the air flow created by the tractor-trailers along the highway caused me to blink.

'Isn't it a little dangerous to hold a flame beneath the gas tank?'

'Don't worry, Dad,' I said, 'I'm not making a bomb. Besides, the gas tank is miles away from the axle.'

'It is, is it?' He kneeled next to me. 'Is that my lighter?'

I nodded. Not only had I not got his permission to use his lighter, I had adjusted the flame of his lighter to maximum so that it hissed like a miniature acetylene torch. He was edgy when he thought you were wasting things, edgy when you left the lights on in the house or didn't turn off the stereo before leaving. I expected him to talk about filial disrespect and property rights and lack of consideration for his belongings and to top it off with another headbanger.

'Lucky I brought some refill fluid,' he said and then sat down in the passenger seat and massaged his ankle, which was dark blue because of a heart problem.

I had to lie under the car to remove the remainder of the plastic. When I was done he lobbed the keys at me.

'Your turn,' he said.

Though the sun was far from setting when we pulled back on to the highway, he told me to turn on the lights. 'Dusk is the most dangerous time to drive,' he said. He switched on a special reading light and from his soft leather briefcase he retrieved the latest issue of the *Monthly Review*. On its cover was an article by someone called Kwame Nkrumah about African independence and another one by Samir Amin on the deformation of the Egyptian state.

'What's the difference between exchange value and use value?' I asked him suddenly. He looked at me. 'No, really,' I continued hastily, 'what good does our knowing about poverty do for the poor themselves?' He smiled. Encouraged, I continued. 'What good are we if we can't set a broken bone, grind sand into glass or electrify a poor man's hut? What good are all these books and journal articles about capitalism in its final stages?'

'Not bad,' he said, looking out of the window and digging

out his pipe. 'Not bad at all.' He studied me. The swelling on my cheek seemed to subside. 'You've been reading. Do you also consider yourself a Marxist?' I nodded vigorously. 'Dangerous, that.' He laughed and ate some Triscuits with cheese we'd bought somewhere between Onandoga Lake and Tioghionoga River; he bent over to gather up some cracker crumbs that had fallen on the floor because, like me, he couldn't enjoy these small pleasures if he knew he had to clean up afterwards.

'OK. Let me try.' He lit his pipe and puffed. The flame dipped into the pipe-bowl. 'We live in a society,' he said, 'where each individual's specialized knowledge is relatively useless, unless there is a critical mass of like others to make us productive. That's only a partial response.'

He put his feet up on the dashboard and his flared pants fell back. A knotty cluster of veins protruded above his darkened ankle as if there was an argument going on about which way his blood should flow. He launched into a lecture that lasted for nearly an hour, during which time my mind wandered, though I nodded seriously as if I understood what he was saying. I concentrated on the highway. We passed a series of telephone poles and the displaced air made a whomp-whomp sound. When I passed a truck there was that moment when I felt we were being sucked into an air bubble. The after-tow slowed us down when we reached the front of the truck and then vroom! we were past it, we'd broken through the invisible barrier, we were now ready to take on the next tractor-trailer.

When he was done speaking to me, he told me he was

especially happy because at my steady eighty miles an hour, we'd be in New York in under three hours.

A few miles outside Manhattan, in the vicinity of Yankee Stadium, we stopped at a Texaco gas station so he could place a call. A hillock of thick bushes made it seem as if the gas station bordered on the edge of some serious New York State wilderness, but this thin slice of untrammelled nature was too small to use for anything else but the back yard of the gas station.

'I've got some news,' he said when he returned, bending down to my open window. I got out of the car. 'They've fallen.'

'Who?'

His eyes were bright and his fists were clenched.

'Students are out in the streets of Athens. The soldiers refused to shoot them.' Then he gave me a grin so wide I thought his teeth were going to jump out. 'What do you think of that, young man?' he said. 'The dictatorship is over!'

In the dim twilight, next to a gleaming red tow-truck, behind a small patch of green on a hillock, with the wail of cars and tyres swishing along Highway 95, we shook hands, not knowing how else we were supposed to celebrate the event, and then, since the handshake seemed a rather paltry response to the end of an era, we hugged and patted each other's backs.

The gas-station attendant, in a red Texaco shirt and dusty jeans, stood with his hands on his hips and stared at us. 'Hey!' he shouted. 'Is it a boy or girl?'

Half an hour later we were rattling over the metal slats of

Triboro Bridge; at the bottom of the bridge we turned right at the Neptune Diner, then drove beneath the subway tracks held up by thick steel girders which ran the length of Broadway. My father grew fidgety: he snapped open and shut the holster cover, played with the glove-compartment handle, and tapped his pipe on the gear-stick. If the dictators had really fallen, he said, we'd see people in the streets, lights inside every apartment building would be blazing and horns would be blaring. 'This looks just like one more night in Astoria,' he said. Cars drove slowly, a woman dressed in white pushed her pram calmly along the sidewalk, and a man with cropped hair held three dogs on a single leash. It was all too ordinary, he said.

We stopped at a phone booth so my father could make another call. He returned and shook his head, leaned against the door and crossed his arms.

'Dad?' He was staring up at the buildings. 'Dad?' He got back in and I drove slowly into the heart of Astoria.

'False alarm,' he said. His face seemed to have stretched a mile. 'They brought out the tanks. One dictator fell, but another one took his place.'

'But you said . . .'

'I was wrong!'

'But at the gas station . . .'

'Shut up!'

'You know what, Dad?' I heard a great crashing sound like the rush of water over the Niagara Falls. 'I'm glad the dictators didn't fall! Do you hear? I'm glad! Glad!' Something had got into me and wouldn't let go. I stopped the car right in the middle of the road. A car honked. 'I'm glad they're torturing people! I'm glad the working class always loses! I'm glad Trotsky was assassinated! I'm glad Stalin won and you can preach to me all you like, I'm still going to be glad! Long live capitalism! You hear me, Dad? Long live capitalism!' I glared at him and folded my arms across my chest. The car drove around us, honking all the while.

I squinted and raised my hands in front of my face.

'I'll drive,' he said and immediately got out of the car, motioned to a Chevy behind us to wait, and came around to the driver's side. I was breathing fast when I slid over the gearstick and plonked myself into the passenger seat. My hands were sweating and my whole body was shaking. He gripped the steering wheel hard, like when we raced past the Dodge Charger, except now he drove slowly.

'I know you don't mean what you said.' He spoke like a patient and slightly exasperated professor. I shrugged my shoulders. He reached out and touched the sore spot on my cheek lightly with his hand, just barely, and nodded his head with his lips pursed and a squint of his eyes.

'What?' I said.

'You know,' he said.

'What?' I heard him draw in his breath.

'OK,' he said, 'I'm sorry.'

His words echoed inside the car. By the time we turned up Thirty-Fourth Street I'd calmed down like one of those unpredictable Aegean winds.

People were bulking around the entrance to the Crystal Palace, walking up the short flight of stairs and through the double glass doors. A man in a pea-jacket and a small cap tight on his head handed out leaflets; three short men with pocked faces who looked like brothers talked loudly. One of them recognized my father, shouted his name, and very soon the group surrounded our car.

Very calmly, in spite of the enthusiasm to which he normally succumbed immediately, my father removed his jacket and in full view undid the straps for his holster, and stashed the gun in the glove compartment. Now that he was among his supporters perhaps that small reminder of his role was no longer necessary. He put on his jacket, patted his pockets to see he was carrying all his pipery and only then eased himself out of the car. Immediately they hugged him, clapped him on the back, kissed him, pulled him into their embrace and shouted in Greek, 'Did you hear about the student uprising? Any deaths?' Not the crowds he was used to, but certainly in numbers great enough to form that critical mass he needed to call himself a leader.

Passing in front of the car, he stopped to straighten the Mercedes symbol, which was tilted backwards, turned his head and stared at me as if he'd suddenly remembered something. He looked like a child who's insisted all winter on being sent to camp, but when he's finally reached the camp gates he suddenly wants to go home. For a moment I let myself believe I had something to do with his awkward, homesick gaze. Then he tugged his jacket, looked away, and made his way up the marble stairs, crowded by Greek-Americans and Greek immigrants with tight shirts and sideburns that reached their chins.

The main room of the Crystal Palace on the second floor was windowless, lit by two large chandeliers; and a large Greek flag hung from the ceiling. Roses were pinned along the edges of the blue and white stripes. The man next to me smelled as if he'd just eaten a whole lamb the way my grandmother used to make it, crammed with her special concoction of salt, pepper and garlic.

My father strode to the podium, stood behind the microphone and gave his jacket to someone, rolled up his white sleeves, dug one hand in his pocket and leaned towards the mike. He no longer looked like a kid going to camp. He was the Pan-Hellenic Liberator.

People applauded. I, too, started to clap but suddenly it seemed incredibly foolish for a son to applaud his father. I folded my arms across my chest and looked around defiantly. I expected someone to ask me, 'Why aren't you applauding?' to which I would answer, pretending to be irritated that my identity had been uncovered, 'Why should I? I'm his son.'

Nobody noticed the fact I wasn't applauding. Outside the Crystal Palace, the subway train droned in the distance and came to a halt with a great frictive shriek. I could pass through the doors, walk down the marble stairs and, for a quarter, ride on the subway into Manhattan. I could hang out in Washington Square and kick a stray can on the sidewalk with my hands in my pockets like a hero in the movies. Who would notice my absence?

My father's voice rose in pitch and I knew from experience, even without listening to what he was saying, that he was reaching an oratorical peak, those crescendos that required as their counterpoint resounding applause from those of us living in the below. After a final cannon-blast of words he paused and pursed his lips, and, in almost a whisper, said the words that capped his first rhetorical flourish. After an initial hesitation and a shiver of revulsion for myself, I joined the thunderous applause, stepping fully into that split-second of silence, a silence which – since he had spent at least fifty thousand dollars to raise me – I believed was my duty to dispel.

After the speech we had dinner with about thirty others at a Greek restaurant on Atlantic Avenue in Brooklyn, where my father explained, while puffing on his pipe and dipping one hand into his jacket like a professor giving a lecture to his devoted students, the present 'constellation' of super-powers and the role of their attendant satellites and why capitalism was the negation of culture. I listened proudly and pretended to preside over the dinner as if I were the chairman, as if these words were things that I was already privileged enough to comprehend.

That night, rather than remain in New York, my father took a night train to Washington so he could 'convene' with other Greek–American organizations early in the morning. From there he would head to Florida, stopping along the way in all the cities with largish Greek populations, and then fly back to Toronto. We shook hands rather formally in front of the small crowd that stood outside the restaurant, and then I got back into the Mercedes and headed towards New England, in the company of four Greeks from Canada who were happy for the ride back to Ontario, and particularly happy at the opportunity to badger me with questions about my father.

They believed I was the most qualified to analyse, in great detail, the deeper meaning of my father's dreams. Perhaps they were right. I don't remember much about the return trip except that they took turns massaging my back while I sprawled across the back seat and told them about the independence of Africa and the degeneration of the Egyptian state. Way before we had reached Niagara I had fallen asleep, succumbing to the warmth and comfort of their laps.

15   *Father Dancing*

Never give a sword to a man who can't dance.
Celtic motto

For years after the night my father was arrested, I continued to have difficulty falling asleep. Absolute silence and absolute darkness were prerequisites. A crack of light was enough to keep me up for hours. Sounds of any kind, Hector coughing in the adjacent room, the toilet flushing, and especially the loud voices of people speaking politics, were anathema. Worse was my expectation of being awoken and the dread that I'd have to start the whole sleep process all over again.

One night, then, in spite of all the hermetic qualities of my room – double-thickness curtains, wall-to-wall carpeting and sealing tape along the edges of the door – a persistent beat filtered upstairs and thumped its stubborn way past all my careful defences. I tried to block the sounds with the pillow over my head (I refused to wear ear-plugs, my mother's suggestion – what if there was a siren or soldiers came into our home at night and I was sleeping?) but that didn't work. Finally I threw the covers off, slipped on my frayed gym shorts, and opened the door. Now I heard the whiny voice of a Greek singer, sporadic clapping, and peculiar rhythms. My mother was visiting her parents in Chicago and my father had turned his small dinner group into a party.

I decided to show up like a kid from hell, half-naked, white legs, skinny body and barefoot – especially barefoot, to shock them with the sight of my maimed left foot. My tousled hair, blinking eyes, and whining, white-fleshed face might gain me sympathy or disgust. Either way, my presence would quash the spirits of the irreverent revellers and allow me to succumb to a deep and thankful sleep.

Walking down the stairs, the music grew louder and I could make out a raspy voice singing, 'Cloudy Sunday/Like my heart.' Strangled bouzouki notes raced wildly between phrases. I arrived at the crest of the sunken living room and saw the source of my discomfort. A number of men and one woman were clapping for a man who was dancing: my father. Forming the circle around him were Angela, his secretary, dressed in a knee-length blouse; Antoni, the Balkan decathlete who performed handstands and who told stories about life in Bolivian shanty towns; Phil, who had left his small village in Northern Greece to become a plumber in Toronto; and Christo, one of my father's university students who also worked at a Greek restaurant on Bathurst Street. Yorgo, fully recovered from torture, squatted on the wooden floor and clapped out the beat. His dark eyes, which helped him get rides from women when he finished work at the Greek radio station in Danforth, seemed to speak of the prison cells from which he had just come. My eighty-year-old grandmother sat on the couch and watched, her feet dangling above the floor.

Being hard of hearing, she didn't seem to realize how loud the party was.

Head down, one hand tucked behind his back, the other holding worry beads, my father moved slowly, with heavy, responsible steps. He swayed like someone drunk. He careened from one side to the other, as if about to fall, lifted himself from a bent position and spun, then crouched and slapped the parquet with both hands, back and forth as if he were sweeping the floor.

The *zebekiko* song speaks of loves lost, of poverty and mistaken choices – it is a song born from life – but the cultural semantics escaped me at the time, for, at the age of fifteen, I had lived in Greece for only a few years and couldn't remember hearing tunes like these nor had I ever seen my father dancing. Canada was now my home. Gone were the days spent collecting golden pine-nuts on Skopellos or olives from our property in Corinth, gone were the trips to Hydra and Spetses, gone were the winters where a flake of snow was a remarkable event. Winters in Canada froze my breath, stretched the skin on my face, stiffened my fingers. By six in the evening the country disappeared into its insulated home to sleep, not to dance in smoke-filled rooms.

Faced with all this Greekness, I realized that it wasn't just sleeplessness that had brought me to the living room. Bottles of wine and ashtrays testified to the excess. The more they clapped, the more I rebelled against the music with its absurd beat, a music whose words by now seemed other-worldly. I was almost embarrassed that I knew enough Greek to understand the gruff voice coming from the stereo. The room was stuffy with sweat, the romance of exile and maleness. It was no longer a matter of getting to sleep.

I walked around the small group, my half-naked presence ignored as if it were natural, and made my way to the other side. Here I contemplated the unthinkable: turning down the volume on the stereo. This was not a university auditorium where turning off the speakers while my father spoke was an accepted and expected protest tactic; this was my father's living room, where sabotage meant betrayal, especially on a night when he was recapturing his special bit of Greece, re-claiming it from exile, thrusting it into this small corner of Canada called King City, Ontario. I twisted the volume knob. The music stopped. So did the clapping and the dancing.

The silence brought them round. Then and only then did they realize I was in the room. They turned towards me in amazement, not yet prepared to connect my presence with the sudden silence, not yet prepared to accept that it was not a power failure or the record skipping or some natural phe-nomenon caused by God, but this ridiculous-looking boy who had switched off the music – this skinny adolescent gazing at them in bright-faced defiance.

Yorgo rose first. He was always one to try and reconcile differences. Conflict hurt his soul, made him sad. But he didn't rush over to turn up the volume nor to scold me. He seemed unsure whether to admonish the son or to hover next to the father, his leader-in-exile, and assuage him. Antoni rubbed his solid chin, flipped his longish hair to one side, and stood back as if better to appreciate the dynamics of the situation; Angela looked right at me with her dark, gentle eyes, telling me in that way to turn the thing back up, for God's sake. For her I almost did. I knew she would pay for my father's foul mood, just as I knew she would defend me if my father, her boss, slapped me across the face. Christo was unable to take his eyes off my maimed foot. Phil looked first at me, then at my father, then back at me. They would not get involved. This was family stuff, and in this family father ruled and the son obeyed, especially such a father, their leader, and such a son, this half-clothed apparition with long hair who looked no better than all those other high-school-aged Canadians, a boy who had no place in this bastion of illusion and exile.

But my father had still not acknowledged me. Though he had stopped dancing, he remained hunched and kept his back turned. I knew he was giving me time to reconsider, to weigh the costs of his torrential wrath against the benefits of my momentary insolence. I imagined him undoing his belt buckle and pulling free his belt, like other times when his anger got the better of him. When the silence persisted, he turned slowly and looked right at me. Angela drew in her breath. The record was still spinning and from it came tiny shouts as if some dwarfish characters were trapped inside the vinyl.

I was quite ready to defend myself. If ordered to turn it up, I would say I needed my sleep – lord knows, the family had heard that one enough times – because of a crucial exam tomorrow. That was when I saw something in his face that surprised me. Perhaps I imagined what I saw, but for a moment I thought I saw pain. Was it the song? Or was it because he saw me as I was, more a Canadian than anything else? Once he spoke it would be too late. Then he would have to punish me. His authority could not be questioned, especially in public. Once the punishment had been meted out, the evening would disintegrate, people would leave, and I knew my father would stomp around alone in his office, puffing on his pipe, guilty and angry.

Suddenly music filled the room. 'Who will mourn for you when you die,' the song asked. There was an audible sigh of relief from Yorgo and Angela, and Antoni tossed his handsome head and clapped his hands. '*Ala!*'

My fingers had turned up the volume.

The whole thing probably didn't last for more than a few seconds. Without even the slightest acknowledgement, not even a nod or a smile, my father bent his head and then stood perfectly still for the short remainder of the song. 'No eyes will cry, no hearts will break.' He was allowing the music to seep inside him, the beat to enter his being, he was collecting his emotions and waiting until the next song began. Then and only then did he begin to turn, slowly, head still bowed. His movements grew heavy; he lifted his right leg and slapped his heel, hard.

And so, though I lived in this country where December decorated the vast forests with blankets of snow and August coloured the days in golden hues, though I lived in this country where summers smelled of freshly cut grass and insect repellent, this country of Arctic loons, wolves and northern lights, I began to listen, slowly, ever so slowly, to music written for a different world and for a hotter climate, music from composers with names that bounced like hard rubber against my mouth when I pronounced them, names like Tsitsanis, Bithikotsis, Hadjidakis, and Theodorakis.

One year later, by which time I'd reached the respectable age of sixteen, democracy, and with it our family, returned to Greece. My father entered politics at the head of his own party and I took time off from my final year in high school to join his electoral campaign. I was as close to being a Canadian as any other boy my age. I had finally become captain of the basketball team, I read Farley Mowat and Robertson Davies, worried about the effects of Quebec separatism on the provinces and kept tally of the number of hat tricks scored by Bobby Orr. The only person who spoke Greek to me all those years abroad was my grandmother, she who had taught me that the letter lambda resembled a boy with a bowed head and that the letter epsilon was as fragile as a dried-out sea-urchin.

On the campaign trail I was suddenly plunged into a Greece I had never known. I followed my father into strange towns that looked nothing like the Cycladic summers of my childhood. Instead of the jubilant men and women who once crowded into our kitchen and loitered outside our house, instead of the charged multitudes of Patras and Athens, instead of villagers rushing out to greet and hug us and wrap us in their strong arms, the people were silent, afraid to talk to us, they lacked passion. What had been done to them?

The other males my age dressed in loose, see-through shirts and hip-hugging pants while I wore baggy corduroys and colourful T-shirts and kept my hair long. I was sure they didn't have hockey on television and didn't know a thing about basketball.

With the men from abroad – Phil, Christo, Yorgo, and a new one, Michali, a Saab factory worker returned from Sweden – we formed part of a fifty-car cavalcade that raced from town to town, spreading the message of socialism. My father would arrive in a village, stand up on the roof of a van, dash off a twenty-minuter with a bull-horn, then plunge on to the next town to dash off another. Between speeches I tried to keep up with my homework. At Phil's home in Kozani I learned that Lord Strathcona pounded the last spike of the Canadian Pacific Railroad on 7 November 1885; in Alexandroupoli I memorized Tsernyshev's law of large numbers and at the Xenia hotel in Arta I read Sophocles' *Oedipus Rex* in English while Michali slept in the bed next to me.

One afternoon we arrived in the port-city of Kavala, and for the first time I was reminded of the summers of my childhood. Old women carried sticks on their backs, old men sat in the cafés and stared at the convoy, donkeys skittered out of the way; tractors carried families, children kicked a home-made ball made of tin foil. Wearing a black leather jacket and green turtleneck – in contrast to the suit and tie of all other politicians – my father that night was particularly inspired. The crowd was good and stretched from the town square all the way to the sea. Large trawlers and small *kaiki* boats were decked out in green flags which ran along their masts. It reminded me of the time my grandfather tamed a crowd as impressive as the rugged mountains of Achaia.

After the speech and a dinner with a hundred or so of the

locals (the dinners were always the same: beef, gravy, French fries and fruit) my father excused himself and returned to his room. Rarely did he acknowledge my presence or make an effort to include me in the activities – but that was nothing new. Though I wanted to be part of the excitement, much of the time I felt like a hanger-on, like an observer of a foreign organization, invited to watch the proceedings. But that night some of those from the cavalcade, particularly a close circle of men who had returned from abroad together, who felt slightly disorientated, decided to go out on the town and they invited me to join them. It was already past twelve but Michali said this was early for where we were going. We drove to a building located in the middle of a farm. The nightclub, Asteria, looked like nothing more than a black cement box. A barrage of sound and smoke assaulted us as we entered. There were no windows. Two men played bouzouki. One had his sleeves rolled up and had tucked a lit cigarette into the fret next to the keys. He was stoned, that much about this kind of life I had learned in Canada.

A bottle of J&B whisky sat squarely in the middle of each table, and we were served a plate of sliced oranges and cinnamon-sprinkled slices of apple. We were shown to our seats in front of a stage occupied by a woman in a flowing purple dress. She swung the microphone cord back and forth, and when the bouzouki finished its lead, she broke in with song: 'The mountains resound as my sorrows abound.'

Her voice seemed a mockery of voices, tremulous, operatic, sometimes low and sultry, other times rising high and shrill, never quite reaching the right note. She wiggled her body, careful not to shake her breasts too much. Michali perched his elbows on the table and laid his chin in his palms, face shining with ecstasy. Phil told me she was a 'professor of love' and wondered if he could be her student. I had never seen such a thing. King City offered only jeaned women, who dieted and exercised, who had upright breasts and wore skirts above the knee, whose hair was fresh and who shouted, 'Hey! How's it hangin'?' At the badly lit Friday-night-in-the-gym affairs they strolled around with beer bottles in their hands and hardly looked at us males. Nor could I imagine them dancing for us. When the singer finished her song, Michali and Phil stood and applauded. She bowed, but only slightly, as if this spontaneous and magnanimous show of enthusiasm were natural, as if we were so much riff-raff not to be taken seriously. She sang another.

When Phil tried to throw some drachma notes at her, she came over, stepped on an empty chair and stood on our table, then gazed at us from her lofty height like a queen. Michali scattered petals over her shoulders and then, clenching a thousand-drachma note between his teeth, brought his face to her feet and tried to tuck the note into her shoe. When she left our table, I stood up and told Michali I wanted to go. He called a taxi and said he'd be returning soon, too. It was nearing daybreak when I heard him fumbling with the keys as he tried to find the lock.

That first night was like the first time you taste a cigarette or sip whisky or down a shot of vodka: it burns and you hate it but for some unknown reason you try again and again and again until finally you want it, you want the burn and the hate.

The taste of night grows on you. So during that campaign, after the final evening speech, it became a habit for a bunch of us to visit such places. They were smoke-filled caves, with the sound up so high that when you left at five in the morning your head buzzed as if you'd stood right up against the monster speaker at a Led Zeppelin concert. If my father's speeches in the villages were full of hope, the words of the songs were saturated with pessimism and abandonment: 'One day on the sidewalk I shall die,' goes one; 'the dawn breaks sweetly atop the mountains, but for me it is dark,' goes another. 'Cry, my bouzouki, cry for the double-sided blade.' Amen.

During that week, when my father rose to speak in the towns, I wondered how the same people who applauded his messages about popular sovereignty and social justice could also jam themselves into these night dens and drink until dawn, waking up bleary-eyed and exhausted, their tongues thick and dry as slippers. These weren't songs of revolution, these weren't political songs, not the kind I had heard in the coffee-houses in Toronto, not the ones written by Theodorakis or Victor Jara, who was killed by Pinochet's men the night of the Chilean coup. The real Greece, the country of my childhood, certainly existed, I just hadn't found it yet.

In these first elections in 1974 after our return from exile my father was soundly trounced, receiving only a small percentage of the vote. We watched the results from party headquarters in downtown Athens. My father smoked cigarettes with dozens of other supporters and grew morose as the evening wore on and the results came in. Mother, Michali and

Angela tried to encourage him and told him that even a small percentage gained him a spot in the Greek parliament and that this was still something. He didn't listen. For the first time I saw him nervous; his eyes shifted, his charm evaporated, his smile vanished, and he was irritated by everything and everyone.

Shouts rose from the street to our floor, calls for my father to appear. These were not supporters but gangs of young men who'd set up camp outside the party headquarters. They waved green ties in the air and hung an effigy of a man in a leather jacket from a green rope. Groups of them roamed the street below and plastered dozens of funeral posters on top of our election billboards. Soon the billboards were full of rows of black crosses announcing the death of my father. Early in the morning, when the streets had cleared, we returned home. He was thinking of leaving Greece and returning to our land of exile, Canada.

Much to my surprise, the following evening he invited me and Hector to join him at a nightclub. With Michali, Phil and Jerry, who had once been my grandfather's chauffeur and was now a fixture by my father's side, we piled into a large Mercedes which someone had lent us upon our return, a gas-guzzling machine that chortled and belched out a stream of white smoke as if it were on fire. My father drove with his head close to the wheel and didn't say a word. The air inside the car was stuffy and the Aegean wind wasn't blowing at all.

We arrived after midnight. Outside the nightclub neon lights lit up a picture of a man with deeply recessed eyes. He was the main attraction. The waiters, seeing my father, gave us front-row seats. Compared to the other joints, the Athenian club was more upscale and sophisticated, clean, with white tablecloths, black-suited waiters, decent lighting. The smoke was thick but there were no fly-strips or open toilets next to the swivel doors to the kitchen. The music was instrumental, played by musicians hidden on the barely lit stage. Mirrors ran along one wall and a spinning ball reflected light as it turned. The clients, who wore silk shirts and gold chains, stared at us with open curiosity as the waiters brought us five baskets of roses and three J&Bs. Politicians didn't visit such nightclubs, especially politicians who called themselves socialists.

Suddenly the instrumentals stopped and there he was, standing in front of us: Tsitsanis. He wore a grey suit, his shirt was open and his face was dark with one day's growth. His eyes seemed to say 'I have lived.' He picked up a bouzouki inlaid with mother of pearl that shimmered in the light and plucked the first chords.

'For the "big guy",' he said in his gruff voice. My father seemed to be staring off in the distance, not even aware, it seemed, that Tsitsanis had dedicated his first song to him. Perhaps he was remembering the calm life of King City when we would inhale the aroma of the freshly mowed lawn like an enormous cup of tea or when the snow covered our house up to the windows and we couldn't open the front door. I didn't expect him to dance. But my father rose and we rose with him. A burly man, apparently certain that this song was for him, stepped on to the dance floor at the same time as my father. An awkward moment passed between them. They looked at each other – there are songs about those who have knifed one another for interfering in this solo dance – and suddenly the other man went down on one knee and joined our half-circle, ready to clap along.

Tsitsanis' bouzouki riffs were sharp and clean. When he began to sing I remembered I had heard this song eons ago, that night in King City. 'Cloudy Sunday,' he sang, drawing out the syllables, 'cloudy like my heart.' My father extended his arms, leaned his body forward, bent his knees and squatted slowly. The movements seemed strained, mechanical and the expression on his face was serious, but soon he was slapping the wooden stage with his hands, forehand and backhand. Legs kept tightly together like a slalom skier's, he held the creases of his trousers with two fingers, the way a woman lifts her skirt to cross a puddle. Tsitsanis leaned the bouzouki down in acknowledgement. The spinning silver globe dotted our faces with freckles of light. The bouzouki riffs, Tsitsanis' piercing voice, the flashing lights, and my father's slow, mesmerizing turns filled the night. Hector and I urged him on, slapping the floor in front of him. '*Eleos!*' we shouted, 'Mercy!'

When the song was over my father didn't return to the table. He remained half-bent, arms out. He wasn't coming up for air. He didn't turn to thank Tsitsanis nor did he smile. Tsitsanis began another one. My father danced again, this time with slower, less acrobatic steps. And when that was over, still another one, again slowly, and one more. Finally he uncoiled his body until he was standing erect and wiped his broad forehead. The sweat had soaked through his shirt. Whatever it was that kept him on the dance floor had now been extinguished. Tsitsanis bowed. My father shook his hand and smiled, a small enigmatic smile. We returned to the table, nibbled on the cinnamon-spiced apples, and waited respectfully until Tsitsanis had finished the set. Then we got up and left. My father never mentioned Canada again.

I lost my insomnia when, ten years later, I entered the Greek military. Sleep at midnight and reveille at five a.m. was enough to break the spine of any sleeplessness. Since then I have learned to sleep anywhere and under any conditions – in the back seats of cars, on the floors of hotels, in small village houses, on the beaches of a lonely Aegean island, under the blaze of lights; I learned to sleep with music, voices, smoke, and shouting; I learned to sleep during speeches.

One night, outside the barracks of Trikala, with one soldier plucking an old bouzouki and others keeping rhythm with their clapping, I suddenly stood, hunched my shoulders, extended my arms, and danced. My movements must have looked strange because I had little support from my left foot. The soldiers stared. I spun and fell to the ground, but got up immediately and continued. I fell a second time, and got up again. When I finished they applauded me. They'd seen my foot in the shower.

Over the years I have discovered my own dancing style: I move slowly, one hand above my head and the other below my waist as if I am carrying a glass pane, a pane that is both heavy and fragile. Sometimes, to keep from falling, I take quick hurried steps and spin my arms like a windmill. I'm lucky. The dance is supposed to be about a man who's drunk, a man who's finding his balance.

Now, the seven-eighths of the *zebekiko* has become part of my soul, the bouzouki rings inside me and stirs me like a cry in the middle of the night, the eastern voices seem inevitable, as if they had been part of me all my life. The music is not music, it is speeches, cavalcades of cars, emigrant workers, crowd-filled squares. Now when I get up to dance – prompted by an urge to bring on a certain sadness and melancholy – what I see in front of me is not the men on their knees clapping, not just the bouzouki players' hands fluttering like wings. I see crowds, I hear speeches, I see my father, dancing.

16   Life in the Below

In August 1975 I find myself in the heart of central Greece, in Karpenissi, at an altitude of 3,000 feet. I'm sitting with my father's supporters in a taverna built into the side of a mountain. The maple trees are thick and sturdy like the ones in Canada and that's probably why I feel at home. Water flows freely down the slopes and every now and then a gurgling sound gushes forth.

On the drive up a villager asked me to help him obtain a permit to disinter his uncle, who, he claimed, was buried in the wrong cemetery. His request reminded me of a visit last year to Distomo, a mountain town nearly wiped out during the German occupation. A woman dressed in black had dragged me to her home to show me her dead son. He was laid out on the kitchen table and looked as if he were sleeping, except for the gold coins in his eyes. The woman insisted I hold his hands but I refused. Now, driving up the mountain-side, I imagine the boy rising up and the coins dropping to the floor like spilled tears. Just before arriving at our destination, I stop the car and plunge my head under a small but powerful waterfall.

The taverna owner serves us fish from 'the sea down below'. He lays the fish out on the table, then slices and squeezes two lemons over the fish, which are striped black from the grill and smell of charcoal.

'Eat,' he says, 'these are fresh as the dawn.'

I begin with my favourite part, the tail, crisp as a potato chip. The tomatoes are sprinkled with oregano and the bread, torn into ample irregular chunks, we dip into olive oil. Soon we're scavenging through piles discarded earlier, sucking at bits of flesh stuck between the bones. Only when it looks like an army of cats sat down for dinner does the owner serve us watermelon.

When we're done with that we rise, hug and kiss each other and promise to return and not to forget him. It's time to sleep. We're parcelled out to homes of local supporters. I follow a stooped old man in an old black suit to a stone house which, like the taverna, is built into the side of the mountain. The home is lit by a single lamp that hangs from a stiff black cord. On the mantelpiece sits a picture of my grandfather in a white suit and, next to him, standing proudly, is my host, at least two generations younger than he is today. A small oil-burning wick lights up the icon of the Virgin.

The house smells of clove – from Kira-Chrysanthi's walnut cake. A pail splashes in a deep well. The old man returns carrying a pitcher of water and a towel and asks me to join him in his small and tidy garden. He pours water over my hands. I wash my face, letting the cool and sweet water drench my shirt and wet the earth.

During his travels around the world, a famous Greek writer

carried with him a clod of earth from his hometown. This wasn't only to remind himself of Greece, but to remind himself to keep his eyes to the ground, to seek the original mud by which man was made. But he developed this habit of looking down at the end of his life. I am at the beginning of mine.

I look out of the window.

Above, the heavens are glittering with stars. The light from these stars won't stop arriving, not for a million years. It's cold but I don't mind. I lay my head back and finally close my eyes.

I see Lydia falling in love with Memo again, but ultimately not marrying him, despite my grandfather's predictions. I see Hector finishing his final years of high school in Greece, suddenly forced to learn ancient Greek and trigonometry. I see him working summers in the pistachio fields in Aegina and maintaining his carefree spirit. Jason campaigns in my grandfather's electoral district, giving speeches, shouldering a large share of the family tradition. My mother is travelling too, beginning to build a woman's network, carving out her own niche. My father, what else, you can find him in some large town, giving a speech from a hotel balcony, lecturing to party members in a restaurant, but always, always surrounded by men. My grandmother stays at home, the same house we grew up in, with her brooches and Victorian pendants. More and more she recites the French and German poems with which my grandfather courted her when they first met. She waits patiently for our sporadic appearance and her ultimate demise, which, fortunately enough, is late in coming.

As for me, everything still seems possible. I am seventeen.